Nick skidded the jeep to a halt on the far side of the curve, out of sight from below.

From a webbed pouch between the seats, he chose three M-34 incendiary grenades and arranged them in the passenger seat. With a new magazine in Wilhelmina, which was back in his leg holster, Carter looked to the Model 12.

When he dropped the jeep's windshield, the space between the left-hand grip and the magazine fitted perfectly down over the round bar at the base of the windshield.

It would serve as a reverse bi-pod of the sub, allowing Carter to fire, release the Beretta without it flopping, and throw the grenades, only to regrip and fire again.

The Killmaster was ready . . .

NICK CARTER IS IT!

"Nick Carter out-Bonds James Bond."
—*Buffalo Evening News*

"Nick Carter is America's #1 espionage agent."
—*Variety*

"Nick Carter is razor-sharp suspense."
—*King Features*

"Nick Carter is extraordinarily big."
—*Bestsellers*

"Nick Carter has attracted an army of addicted readers . . . the books are fast, have plenty of action and just the right degree of sex . . . Nick Carter is the American James Bond, suave, sophisticated, a killer with both the ladies and the enemy."
—*The New York Times*

FROM THE NICK CARTER
KILLMASTER SERIES

NICK CARTER

KILLMASTER

Night of the Warheads

CHARTER BOOKS, NEW YORK

NIGHT OF THE WARHEADS

A Charter Book/published by arrangement with
The Conde Nast Publications, Inc.

PRINTING HISTORY
Charter Original/June 1984

ISBN: 0-441-57502-1

Charter Books are published by The Berkley Publishing Group,
200 Madison Avenue, New York, N.Y. 10016
PRINTED IN THE UNITED STATES OF AMERICA

*Dedicated to the men of the
Secret Services of the United
States of America*

ONE

Nick Carter stood at the villa's massive upstairs window, gazing out at the softly falling snow. Smoke leaked from the corner of his mouth as his powerful shoulders shrugged deeper into the expensively cut white dinner jacket.

In the villa's great room, behind and below where he stood, the gentle tinkle of china and silverware being set wafted up to his ears.

The table was being prepared for the dinner party Nicholas Carstocus was giving that evening.

"Just a small gathering, select people, to celebrate my liberation from American taxes and the anniversary of my first month in the delightful little principality of Andorra!"

That's what he had told her.

Far below him, headlights pierced the darkness on the road leading up from Andorra-la-Vella, the country's capital.

It's been quite a month, Carter thought, raising a glass of the harsh local red wine to his lips.

And tonight may put the icing on what had started out to be a "piece of cake" mission. Some you figure wrong. . . .

The powerful little sports car slid to a halt in the courtyard below. The engine cut off abruptly, and the driver's side door opened to reveal a vision in white.

But Carter barely saw her. He was already halfway down the stairs and heading across the great room. He deposited the empty wineglass and his cigarette on a table in the foyer, and threw open the massive, copper-studded door.

She stood, smiling, her finger poised about to ring the bell.

"Señorita de Nerro. I am delighted you're here."

"Señor Carstocus."

Her white-gloved arm came up with the expertise and experience of her class. Carter accepted the long, tapering fingers in his and gently brushed the back of the glove with his lips.

His eyes meandered up from the white pumps, taking in the well-shaped legs and hips under the black and white silk dress. Her shoulders were encased in a white ermine stole that was deliciously parted in front to reveal the deep-cut vee of her bodice and the ample swell of her barely concealed breasts.

His eyes then found hers.

"Nicholas, please . . . Nick would be even better."

Her smile broadened across even, white teeth. "And I would prefer Armanda."

"So be it," Carter said, stepping aside and lifting the stole from her shoulders as she passed by him into the foyer.

She was a tall woman, especially for a Latin. Her very long, very dark hair, where it now caressed her bare shoulders, had reddish highlights and just enough of a natural curl to make it bounce delightfully as she moved.

Seeing the empty room, she paused and slipped into a three-quarter turn.

"I am early?"

"Not at all. I told you it was to be a very *small* dinner party."

Realization flooded her high forehead and black, doelike eyes. "How small?"

"For two," Carter replied with a grin, passing the stole to

a woman servant who had soundlessly appeared.

A low, throaty laugh erupted from Armanda's slender throat. "I am not surprised. Since your arrival in Andorra you have established quite a reputation as a man of wealth, mystery . . . and debauchery!"

"But, my dear Armanda," Carter said, his eyes brazenly raking the bulges of satiny flesh above her neckline, "aren't those the very reasons you accepted my invitation?"

Her eyes met his in an unwavering gaze. "Of course." And again the laugh that sent a little quiver up Carter's spine.

Here was a woman of thirty who had debauched through every capital of Europe. A woman whose arts of seduction were legend and whose lovers had been cast aside, broken in heart and wallet.

And she was practically admitting that the very traits she had just laid on Carter were the traits that made him attractive.

It was going to be quite an evening.

"Drink?"

"Wine, please," she said. "But French. The local stuff turns my stomach."

Carter requested a bottle of French white by name and year from the old servant woman, who nodded and slipped away as soundlessly as she had arrived.

"The balcony?" Carter said, gesturing to the stairway. "There is an excellent view of Andorra-la-Vella, as well as the great room of the villa."

"Enchanting."

Carter moved his forearm under her hand, and together they mounted the stairs.

The snow had lightened a little now, and as was so often the case in the high mountains, there were breaks in the overcast that allowed some moonlight to pour through and illuminate the landscape.

The lights of Andorra-la-Vella and its sister village across the narrow river, Les Escaldes, burned like so many tiny beacons through the intermittent flakes of whiteness. Beyond the two villages, the valley stretched in peaceful slumber upward to the majestic white-capped peaks that surrounded it on all sides.

"It's a beautiful country," Carter whispered at her shoulder.

She nodded, her strong chin and aristocratic nose barely bobbing. "Do you know what Napoleon said when he decided to bypass Andorra in 1804?"

"No."

" 'It is too amazing to invade. Let it stand as a museum piece!' "

Carter smiled but did not reply as the little Spanish woman scurried up the stairs with a tray, left it at Carter's side, and departed.

Yes, perhaps Bonaparte had bypassed Andorra in his conquest of the world. But someone—perhaps the Russians, perhaps one of the more powerful and ambitious Third World countries—had decided to invade the tiny principality in a more modern way.

That was Nick Carter's mission: find out who was suddenly interested in Andorra, find out what they were doing, and stop them.

"To Andorra," Armanda de Nerro said, turning to Carter and raising her glass.

"And beauty," Carter replied, lightly touching her glass to create a perfect ringing sound.

She sipped the wine and studied Carter's rugged features over the rim of the glass.

"You are Greek?"

"Greek-American," Carter replied and went on to let his memorized cover story unfold. "I was born and raised in New York City, and lived there most of my life. About two years ago I emigrated to Paris."

"And now you live in Andorra."

"Not quite. I'm taking a long vacation to see if the climate suits me. This villa is leased for six months."

Armanda slipped her eyes from his and turned back to the falling snow.

"And you?"

"I live in Andorra so I can be near my own country."

"Spain?"

"Yes."

"But why don't you just live in Spain?"

Her lovely dark head sagged slightly. "That, *señor*, is a very long story."

"I'd like to hear it," Carter said and thought, *to see if it agrees with what I already know!*

Her dark eyes came up to fasten intently on his. "And I, Nick, would like to hear why you left the land of plenty, the United States."

"*Touché*," Carter said and reached for the bottle to refill their glasses. "Perhaps, Armanda, before this evening is over, we will learn a great deal about each other."

"Perhaps."

Her smile was like a thousand lights coming on at the same time. But oddly, Carter thought, it would not melt a single ice cube.

"I seem to remember the name . . . Carstocus. Athens, I think . . ."

Carter returned her steady gaze with a slight smile curving his lips. He offered no enlightenment.

"Ah, yes, I remember now! A self-styled general. He was the leader of a band of rebel Communist guerrillas at the end of the war. He slaughtered Greeks and Germans alike as the Allies swept through Greece toward Bulgaria."

Carter's smile broadened, but he did not alter the flat, noncommittal expression in his eyes. The woman was testing him. She had probably been briefed some time that day, or perhaps the day before, on his background and the story of Constantin Carstocus.

She was baiting him, and this time Carter replied.

"My uncle. He was eventually shot as a Communist rabble-rouser."

"But you had no connection with him?"

"None," Carter replied. "Indeed, quite the opposite. My father was very different from his brother, very immersed in capitalism. I only *know* of my uncle. I never *met* the man."

"I see. That is a pity. From the stories I have heard, he must have been quite a man."

"Perhaps. His name was rarely spoken in our house."

"Then you do not approve of your uncle's politics?"

There it was, an open question. But Carter was saved from answering her for the time being.

"Señor Carstocus?" The dark-haired little woman stood at the head of the stairs.

"*Si*, Estrellita?"

"Dinner, *señor*, is served."

"*Gracias*," Carter said and turned to his guest. "Shall we?"

Armanda de Nerro glided against him until her firm breasts were pressed to his chest.

She was indeed tall, tall enough that she had only to tilt her head to bring her lips to his.

It was a seething kiss, full of passion and promise.

And Carter returned it in kind until she gently pulled away.

"An appetizer," she breathed, barely parting her lips.

"And, I hope, an omen," Carter replied, "of things to come."

"We shall see," Armanda said, her voice husky and full of sensuality.

Carter followed her swaying hips down the stairway with a

curve to his lips that was more sneer than smile.

Yes, indeed, it had been quite a month since he had staked out a beach three thousand miles or more west of the tiny principality of Andorra.

Quite a month, with a lot of bodies in between . . .

TWO

The eyes were like black ice behind the hooded lids. They seemed somnambulant, but they digested every twitch, every movement on the moonlit beach two hundred yards below.

There were eight of them, crouched in two groups on the sand. A few smoked, the fireflies at the ends of the cigarettes glowing behind cupped hands. Two more—flanked to the right and left of the hill-dweller—served as back watchers for the men on the beach.

Nick Carter's trained ears and the icy eyes had already made their position in the rain forest behind him.

From below there was conversation, hushed and muted, but the distance was too great for the black-clad observer to catch more than an occasional word.

But accents he did catch, allowing conclusions.

They were multinational. Probably few of them spoke more than their native tongue and English. So they were communicating in English, heavily accented by Spanish, French, and Italian.

They had moved in just after sundown, two at a time, all from different directions.

Their dress was the baggy, white overblouse and trousers

of the Yucatecan peasant. When they slipped out of the jungle, there had not been a weapon in sight. But shortly after taking up a position on the beach, hardware had appeared from beneath their clothing and out of the shoulder-slung woven bags at their hips.

Most of it was old stuff: M-1 carbines and Enfields that looked as though they were as old as the Bedouin wars when Rommel's tanks rumbled.

The small irons were Smith and Wesson .38s. It took one hell of a shooter to bring anybody down for good with one of those. It has been said that the best way to take a man out with one was to throw it at him.

The newest thing showing was a Beretta Model 12 sub.

Carter had already made a mental note that the head guy with the Beretta would be the first to go. Not just because of his hardware, but because of who he was.

Nels Pomroy, CIA, retired. At least on the books.

In actual fact, Pomroy had decided—upon his retirement two years before—to go into business for himself, using the expertise and contacts he had gained while working for the Company.

He had become a broker for various international assassins around the world.

You want a businessman or politician gunned down somewhere? Just contact old Nels. For a solid percentage of the fee he would find you the man for the job.

And when the killing business was slow, Pomroy had a second, even more profitable sideline: arms sales.

That was his current business that night on a Mexican beach.

Carter's assignment was to stop the arms shipment and, more importantly, put Nels Pomroy out of business . . . permanently.

He had become a big fat embarrassment to his former employers.

It would not be much of a contest. In contrast to the men on the beach, Carter bristled with the latest.

A close-action Beretta 9mm pistol was leathered beneath his left armpit, the snout of its silencer tickling his lower left side.

His favorite Luger, Wilhelmina, had been left behind on this assignment.

Reason?

All the hardware Carter carried would be destroyed when the job was over. AXE chief David Hawk had been explicit on those instructions.

"No trace, N3, not even a shell casing. I want it as if you or them had never been there."

A Beretta 93R machine pistol hung low, Western-style, on his right hip. Its leather had been customized with a plastic, friction-reducing lining.

The 93R had also been customized away from factory specs. A suppressor had been installed, as well as machined springs designed to cycle the cartridges.

They made the Beretta a quiet killer.

At his side rested one of Lt. Col. Uziel Gal's finest: a Galil assault rifle. It had been modified to fire 5.56 shells with the same accuracy and reliability as its big-brother predecessor, the AK-47. Firepower was more than adequate with an elongated Stoner Mag holding forty-nine slugs in the magazine and one napping in the chamber waiting to be awakened.

And for icing he had infrared eyes to see the slugs on their way, goggles so that his hands were free to do the job.

Carter let his eyes float. Quintana Roo territory, Yucatán Peninsula, Republic of Mexico. A soft sand beach, isolated, desolate, fronting many miles of muggy, steam-sweating tropical jungle and rain forest.

Not a very pretty spot, he thought with a grimace, but as good as any place to die.

"They call themselves Latinos for Freedom. It's a small group and not affiliated, so until now we haven't paid them a hell of a lot of attention."

David Hawk paused to sip from the cup of steaming coffee in his right hand.

They were in Hawk's office in the Amalgamated Press and Wire Services building, Dupont Circle, Washington, D.C.

Hawk's right hand returned his cup to the table. The left, holding a cigar, came up. The rope's well-chewed end split his lips and found a groove between his teeth.

"As near as we can tell, Latinos for Freedom are rebel rebels. They raise random hell, with all sides as targets. A bomb here, a raid there. Hell, they even assassinated one right-wing tinhorn dictator, then turned right around and tried to nail the socialist who succeeded him!"

Until now, Carter had sat silently, smoking, digesting his boss's every word and storing it in the computerlike memory bank of his mind.

Now he asked questions.

"Unrest for unrest's sake?"

"That's it. We couldn't pin them down and, God knows, we've got enough trouble down there anyway, so we ignored them. The Russians and Fidel left them alone because unrest is the name of their game as well. Hell, they were giving our side as much trouble as they were giving the Marxist rebels, so the Communists figured, let 'em play."

"But now they've joined the worldwide terrorist fraternity."

"Looks that way," Hawk said, chewing his rope thoughtfully. "It happens. The Irish IRA provos get together with the Italian Red Brigade. The Palestinians help out the rebel Turks. It's all an exchange of favors."

"So we nip the Latinos for Freedom in the bud before they form a coalition?"

"Right," Hawk replied. "And there's another reason. Remember Nels Pomroy?"

Carter's teeth came down hard on the filter tip of his cigarette. "Yeah, I know him, and about him."

"He's the man," Hawk said. "We want him . . . dead. We think he's brokering this deal for the Basque terrorists. It's probably some kind of a trade-off; we don't know. But the best way to stop it is to get Nels and the arms."

Carter mashed his cigarette. "When and where?"

"The goods are on the way now, a Libyan freighter, the *Star of Tripoli*. She ETAs sometime tomorrow night at Marianao, Cuba."

"Cuba?" Carter asked. "I thought you said they weren't Fidel-backed . . ."

"They're not. No aid there. It's strictly a deal between the Basques and the Latinos for Freedom. Fidel's probably just turning his head and letting a little import-export happen in his port."

"Like a way station," Carter added.

"Exactly. The hardware's end-use certificate states Nicaragua, for defense. We all know that's a crock. We think the goods will be trucked from Marianao overland to Cabo San Antonio. From there it's night-ferry time to the Yucatán. The landing spot is an inlet about twenty miles south of Punta Herrero. I've got the coordinates."

Carter closed his eyes and conjured up a map in his mind. His voice, when he spoke again, was a low monotone relaying what his eyes saw on the back of his lids.

"The Yucatán channel, at that point, is about a hundred

and twenty-five miles wide from the tip of Cuba to the edge of Quintana Roo.''

"Right," Hawk came back. "A piece of cake for a *contrabandista* who's good with a sail and a tiller."

"When?"

"We figure day after tomorrow. We're guessing ETA around midnight or a little before, so the movers can get back to Fidel-land before dawn."

"Any particulars besides making sure delivery doesn't go down?"

A worried frown crossed Hawk's forehead but quickly disappeared as a chuckle rolled from his thick throat.

"Stopping delivery and getting Pomroy is the main thrust, but I'd be a damned fool if I thought you wouldn't want to follow through on anything you find, N3."

"Like, what's the favor the Basques want done for the arms payment?"

"That would be a big help."

Carter became silent, scrutinizing everything Hawk had told him and his own thoughts. When it was all ID'd, catalogued, and filed, he opened his eyes and spoke again.

"I'll try for a prisoner."

"It would help," Hawk said, "but not enough for a risk, if you know what I mean. Top priority is the arms, Pomroy, and secrecy. I wouldn't want you left dead and the mess not cleaned up."

"Right. How do I go in?"

"Private flight to Mérida. No problem with ordnance that way. A jeep will be waiting. Any questions asked, you're a sisal buyer from Hamilton Hemp Industries, Dallas. I've got papers."

"I'll want to be on the beach by dawn day after tomorrow, before they recon or come in."

"No problem. But all day in that jungle? It'll be hotter'n hell."

"I've been there before."

Then Carter smiled.

"Besides, comes the night, it will be even hotter."

Carter stretched without making a sound or moving a leaf of the damp-seeping green canopy shielding him.

It had been one hell of a wait since before dawn that morning to . . .

The chronometer on his left wrist read 2235 hours.

If Hawk's guess was right—and there was little doubt in the Killmaster's mind that it was—the arms boat would be sliding in soon.

Movement on his right flank about a hundred yards to the rear. It was quickly followed by the same sounds to his left.

He tensed momentarily and then, just as quickly, relaxed.

It was feeding time for the mules who had been brought to form a pack train.

Soon it was quiet again, only the sound of the lapping waves breaking the stillness.

He waited until 2300 hours.

And then it came, a blinker light from about a mile out.

Three longs, two shorts, and three more longs.

Movement and subdued shouts from the men on the beach. One of them angled a high-power flash toward the sea and repeated in kind.

Ten minutes later a sail materialized against the gray horizon. Even as Carter watched, the canvas was dropped and furled by scurrying men.

And then the steady *chug, chug, chug* of an inboard reached his ears. As the sound grew louder, the boat loomed larger.

It was a thirty-foot shrimper with cranes port, starboard, and aft. Normally those steel arms would be used to trail in nets and lift Neptune's nourishment aboard the craft.

But tonight they would be used to unload crates of death.

The skipper was good. He reversed the boat's screw at just the right time to let bow and keel nuzzle the beach. The boat had barely stopped yawing when both port and starboard cranes went into action.

Ready hands waited, and Carter could hear the grunts and gasps as they sloshed through the surf with the hardware.

Two of the eight men on the beach split off, moving back into the trees.

Carter guessed they had been dispatched to bring the mules. Minutes later the guess was confirmed when the two men reappeared. Each of them led a string of ten mules in his wake.

It was time to start the game.

Carter secured his mind, blocking out everything but the moment.

Like a dark shadow, Carter glided to his feet. He slung the Galil over his shoulder and adjusted the lanyard until its muzzle was just nudging his right hip.

Then, with the infrared-lensed goggles in place over his eyes, he moved out.

Like a formless, silent ghost, he slithered through the dense undergrowth.

The flanker to his right looked bored. He lounged against a tree listening to the action on the beach. An old Enfield was cradled in his arms like a sleeping babe.

With a whisper, Carter rescued Hugo, his pencil-thin stiletto, from its sheath on his right leg.

The sentry was a heartbeat away from hell when he sensed Carter's presence. His head was just turning when the vise of Carter's left arm encircled his throat.

The head came up and back as the needle of steel found flesh.

The only sound was a gurgling rasp.

One down, a limp bundle of white slipping to the jungle

floor, the front of his blouse crimson.

The body had barely settled in death before Carter was moving again.

The forest was quiet, with little wind rustling the trees. Now and then an animal scurried away from the swiftly moving shadow.

But even the little jungle native, slithering in fear, made more noise than Killmaster N3.

Flanker number two was standing dead center in a wide clearing. His rifle was cradled carelessly in his left arm as his hands fumbled with the zipper on his fly.

He had just relieved himself . . . for the last time.

In one motion Carter sheathed the stiletto, dropped to a crouch at the edge of the clearing, and slid the silenced Beretta from under his left arm.

Without knowing death was waiting, the guy took three steps toward Carter.

Only two while he was still alive.

A 240-grain slug made bone chips out of his sternum, leaving a fist-sized hole in the middle of his chest. His mouth made an ''O'' and his eyes went wide with shock.

They were still open when he pitched face forward into the jungle steam.

First and second hits, Carter thought, *but this was only the beginning*.

He now moved in a zigzag pattern, as silently as ever, toward the beach.

Over half the loading was already done. Only six mules still had bare backs. Slung over the other beasts were oilskin bundles.

They worked quickly, efficiently, in teams: two uncrating, four loading the mules, and two dumping the wooden crates into a deep pit they had dug on the jungle's edge.

Staying fifty yards inside the shadowed foliage, Carter

maneuvered parallel to the beach until he was on a straight line with the pit. Then he bore to his left until the toes of his boots hit sand.

The two crate bearers plodded up the beach toward him, their arms loaded. When they were at the very edge of the pit, Carter stepped from the shadows.

"That you, Carlos?"

"*Sí*," Carter growled.

The Beretta wheezed, sending a slug dead center into the man's face. It disintegrated and joined the back of his skull as he pitched forward into the pit.

"*Madre de Dios*," the other one gurgled, clawing for the holstered antique at his hip.

He was rolling to the side as Carter fired again. The Beretta's first slug caught him in the right shoulder, spinning him all the way around. Carter stitched two in the back of his neck, but he was not quick enough.

The Mexican managed to get out a yelp, as much in surprise as pain, just before he died.

It was just loud enough to alert his companions thirty yards away. Carter dived into the trees just as they opened up behind him.

All hell had busted loose, maybe too soon, but Carter knew he would just have to make the best of it.

Four away, six to go.

The firing increased from the beach, all centered on where the eerie, goggled figure had been.

Now he was moving, literally crashing through the heavy undergrowth, back to his original starting point on the high ground. The concentrated firing of the carbines and the .38s covered the sound of his movement. Deftly he leathered the Beretta and rolled the Galil off his shoulder.

By the time he reached the sniper site, he had unclipped the

Galil's folding stock from the military webbed belt around his middle. Ten seconds after dropping to his belly in the already trampled foliage, the stock was in place and the folding bipod was uncorked from under the barrel.

With the shoulder butt nuzzled, Carter reached forward and used his thumb to flip up the night-sight.

The Galil was ready, fifty rounds' worth, with an additional hundred rounds in the two spare magazines hanging from Carter's belt.

The Galil was fitted with a flash suppressor, so he figured he was good for a mag and a half—maybe a full two—from this spot before they made him.

If there was anybody left to do the making.

With the Galil swinging easily on the bipod, he did a fast scan.

Now it was a waiting game. They were quiet after the first shock of assault. Two had dived behind a jagged claw of rocks near the water. Nels Pomroy was precariously peering out from between two of the remaining crates. He was the one with the Beretta sub, the one Carter knew he should have gotten first. But the logistics had been wrong.

So be it.

The remaining three had charged a few feet into what they thought was the protective darkness of the trees.

Between the Galil's night-sight and the goggles, Carter made two of them at once: one partially hidden behind a tree, the other moving straight inland in a half crouch.

He lined through the rear, flip-type ''L'' sight, and squeezed off a burst, and then another.

Only one was needed. It stitched the guy from his navel to his neck.

There was very little sound and hardly any flash.

Just a very quiet death from out of the darkness.

The man behind the tree started firing wildly. He got off five, all harmless, before his old piece gave up the ghost and jammed.

With a shouted curse he dropped the rifle and sprinted for the beach.

Why, Carter didn't know.

But then he didn't care either.

Five feet into the open moonlight, Carter turned the back of the runner's white shirt blue.

A foot farther, it turned a dull, dark red. Cloth shredded and flesh exploded as the lifeless form tumbled into the sand and rolled.

"They got Julio and Ortega!"

"I can see, goddamnit!"

"How many are there?"

"How the hell do I know? I only saw the one!"

All this shouted from the rocks to the crates and back again.

Movement behind the rocks.

Carter sprayed them with a long burst and then another. Chips flew everywhere and all movement ceased.

The third man, who had hit the trees, had now zeroed in on Carter's position. Carter could hear him moving in, belly down, from the left flank.

Carter made the Galil jump, sending slugs into the air and sand on both sides of the crates. It wouldn't do to fire directly into them and try for the man with the sub, Pomroy.

If one crate went, they might all go, taking Carter with them.

The flank prowler was close now. Carter flipped the magazine catch and tossed the near empty slug container into the darkness.

The guy with the sub opened up immediately on the sound, far to Carter's right.

Leaving the Galil, Carter slithered backward, snakelike, out of his sniper spot. Ten feet back he halted, unsheathing the Beretta pistol, waiting.

Thirty seconds. A minute. Two minutes.

The stillness seemed to hang, straining, on a thread.

Then he came, the searcher, belly down, a .38 in his nervous right hand.

Through the goggles Carter could see the shock in his dark face when he discovered the unmanned Galil.

The guy was no commando. He holstered the .38 and went for the Galil.

Carter was on him the second he was over the gun. The butt of the Beretta came down on his skull just behind his right ear.

One grunt and he folded.

Carter checked his pulse. Even, steady. He had a deep gash where the Beretta had hit him, but he would live.

Carter had his prisoner.

He lifted the man's .38 and sent it after the spent magazine.

More random fire from the beach.

Snapping a new magazine onto the Galil, Carter moved out to his left. Forty yards later he angled toward the beach. Just short of the sand, still in heavy cover, he hunkered down.

Effortlessly he relaxed, letting all the strain of the firefight flow out of his muscles.

He would lie like that, unmoving, barely breathing, totally alert, for as long as it would take.

A half hour passed, then an hour.

"Hear anything?"

"Nothing."

Another fifteen minutes.

"There are just the three of us left?"

"Looks that way."

Total patience. Just like a stalking cat.

"André, go for the trees. We'll cover you."

"Jesus . . ."

"Do it!"

André leaped from the rocks like a frightened rabbit, legs churning all the way across the sand. He hit the trees with a crash and plowed inland.

Carter let him go.

André was no more silent than his predecessors had been. Carter could hear every move he made.

Another half hour went by.

"Dead, all of them, except Tito," came André's voice from fifty yards in. "He's zapped, out cold."

"Any sign of the gunner?"

"Nothing."

The remaining guy behind the rocks and Pomroy with the sub moved cautiously out from cover. With equal caution, André emerged from the trees.

"He must have skipped."

"Or we hit him and he's in there somewhere dead."

Carter smiled.

"C'mon, let's get the mules together!"

"Jesus, can we still make Pakolo?"

"If we hurry."

Carter waited until all the mules had been rounded up and tethered in a long line. When this was done he moved out, hugging the ground.

All three of them were near the lead mule, bunched.

"You can live or die," Carter said, low and hard.

They reacted as one, hands clawing for pistols and rifles.

Carter cut the first one nearly in half with a figure eight from the Galil's snout, then tracked right on to number two. He bought it with a fist-sized pattern of 5.56s in his gut.

Pomroy got off one slug that zinged the air where Carter had been. But Carter had already lunged to his right, hit, rolled, and come up firing.

Resignation seemed to fill Pomroy's face just before a solid burst worked its way up over his chest and tore most of his head off.

Carter stood, breathing deeply.

The beach was silent now. Once again only the gentle lapping of the Caribbean broke the stillness.

One by one he gathered up the dead.

There was not a shred of ID on any of them, not even on Pomroy, but that was no more than Carter expected.

Pomroy had five thousand American dollars in big bills and what looked to be a map.

Carter pocketed the money and the map, and then photographed the faces that were still intact enough to be recognizable.

When that was done, he rolled all of them into the pit they had dug to bury the crates.

Weird, he thought, but poetic. They had dug their own grave.

Next he unloaded the mules and wrote down a complete inventory of the arms. When this was done, he dumped everything in the pit on top of the bodies. Then he moved back into the trees to collect the one he had clouted, the one the others had called Tito.

The man was gone.

Somehow he had managed to pull himself together and move out. Carter tracked him over a mile inland to a narrow, one-lane dirt road.

He hadn't quite made it to a one-and-a-half-ton, canvas-covered truck.

Carter checked. The pulse was gone, and he saw why. A blue-black lump just behind his ear had ruptured with the exertion of his run. Had he stayed put, the concussion would have partially passed. As it was, he practically killed himself.

Carter took a quick photo of his face and carried him back to the pit. It took him two more hours to fill in the gaping hole and make the beach look as if it had never been disturbed.

Completely finished at last, he headed inland at a fast jog. It was almost dawn when he reached the jeep and headed out.

All in a night's work, he thought, lighting a cigarette.

But somehow, in the back of his mind, he knew that there would be a phase two.

THREE

Carter stood, silently surveying the table piled high with photos and documents. He was dressed in tan slacks and shirt under a lightweight safari jacket. To his right was David Hawk, and on his left, an undercover operative from Spanish internal security, Ramon Cubanez.

They were in the basement of the National Palace in Madrid, Spain. This section of the basement was the enclave of a special task force that had been set up in the last year to halt Spain's internal terrorist activities.

It all fit, loosely, but it did fit.

Identities had been made from the photos of the dead men. Two of them had been made as members of a Basque revolutionary movement. The rest were Latinos for Freedom members.

Through a lot of groundwork, they had come up with the method whereby the Latinos meant to pay for the arms.

Assassination.

But who? That, for the moment, had them stumped.

"All right," Hawk growled, an unlit cigar clamped tightly in his chiseled jaw. "Let's go over the whole damned thing again."

A six-man suicide squad had been dispatched from South America even before Carter had ruined the arms delivery.

Their final destination was Spain, but where? Spain was a big country.

The fact that they were in the country and had their target was enough. Just because their arms delivery had been screwed up would not stop them from fulfilling their part of the bargain. It was a face-saving kill.

But again the questions. Who? And where?

The map, a scaled-down version of the area around the Manzanal Mountains in northwestern Spain, was a clue.

"My guess is," Hawk said, "that the map you lifted is the key."

"I agree," Carter said, nodding, "but there is nothing there but wilderness and three tiny villages. I doubt that the Basque terrorists would go to all the trouble of bringing in outside guns to kill a local small-town mayor or police official."

"I think you are right," Ramon Cubanez said. "Although they have done it before, I do not think that is the case now."

The Spaniard had barely finished speaking, when the beeper on his belt went off.

"Let us hope this is it," he said, already heading for the door.

Carter and Hawk stood, silent with their own thoughts, until the man returned.

"We might have it," Cubanez said, beaming. "The target could be Julio Mendez, and the place could be . . . here!"

Cubanez stabbed a finger at the map in the center of the table.

The young Spaniard's fingernail was resting on a place called Pakolo.

The sun beat down on the dusty street like a blowtorch from the blue-domed sky.

The intelligence on Pakolo had been right on the nose.

High in the Manzanal Mountains, the tiny village seemed as if it had sprouted from another world, an ancient one. Adobe shacks with tin roofs spread randomly over jagged hills and hung precariously on steep cliffsides.

In the village proper, narrow alleys ran like frightened serpents from the main, dirt street.

The hotel was four tiny rooms above a bar. It fronted what served as the village square. From where Carter sat, sipping thick coffee, a false-fronted line of small stores faced him on the other side of the square. Beyond these, more tin-roofed shacks ambled up a steep hill to the Catholic church and a small monastery nearby.

The square itself was a fifty-by-fifty area that contained the only grass in sight. In its center sat a statue of some long-forgotten hero, and beside it a small platform had been erected.

It was from this platform that Julio Mendez would make his plea for votes in . . .

Carter's chronometer read 1140 hours.

In twenty minutes, give or take.

Beneath the light safari jacket, the short-sleeved shirt he wore stuck fast to his skin with perspiration. Sweat also ran freely between the skin of his right leg and the 9mm Luger strapped to it.

Just to the left of the rickety porch where Carter lounged, sat the jeep he and Ramon Cubanez had driven up from Astorga the night before. Beneath its two front jump seats, under a sheet of canvas, was a 9mm Beretta Model 12. The sub was carrying a forty-round feeder, and two more full magazines nestled under Carter's armpits beneath his jacket.

Using that model had been at the instigation of Ramon Cubanez. It was light, 6.6 pounds, short, a little over sixteen inches with the stock folded, and it delivered at 550 rpms for good accuracy up close.

But Cubanez had an even more elemental reason for its use.

"The Model Twelve is popular among terrorists in Spain. If we use them and all does not go according to plan, no one can come down on my government for wanton killing. It will be construed as terrorist faction against terrorist faction."

And therein, as far as they could figure it, was the heart of the caper.

Cubanez's department had pieced everything together once they guessed that Julio Mendez was the target and that the tiny village of Pakolo was to be his place of execution.

The Euzkadi Ta Askatasuna—or ETA—had long been the Basque revolutionary movement for independence from Spain. Recently, the leadership within the ETA had split on philosophy.

One side—headed by Julio Mendez—wanted a halt in the use of terrorism and wanton killing. The other side wanted terrorism in Spain escalated.

Mendez himself had come out of the closet and was legally running for office in the northern Basque provinces.

It was a tricky proposition. A lot of Mendez's people were behind him, but his rivals in the Basque movement wanted him dead. It was also no secret that several high-ranking officers in the Spanish military did not trust him and would also have liked him dead.

Carter lit his tenth cigarette of the day and cast an eye up over his left shoulder toward the second story of the building behind him.

For backup, Cubanez was directly above him in one of the hotel's front corner rooms.

With a second Beretta sub, he could cover the square itself

and the main drag and alleys to his left all the way to the end of the village.

They were ready, Carter and Cubanez, even if the Madrid military and the regional Guardia Civil were not.

Through State, Hawk had warned the officials in Madrid that something might be coming down that day in Pakolo.

Beyond giving Mendez two bodyguards, the military had chosen to ignore the warning.

It was as if they truly did want him dead.

Maybe they did.

Latin politics is a strange creature.

But the local version of law and order had listened a little better. His name was Hubanyo, and he had listened to every word Cubanez had said.

This end of Basque country around the Manzanal Mountains was Mendez country, and Hubanyo did not want the people's choice wasted on his turf.

He agreed to every suggestion Cubanez rattled off in the local dialect, including the one Carter was most worried about.

The word went out to every man, woman, and child in the village. When the church bells rang noon to herald Señor Mendez's arrival in Pakolo . . . stay home!

Now, other than a few stray, yipping dogs, and Hubanyo's two undersheriffs lounging near the speaker's platform, the street was deserted.

Carter breathed a sigh of relief. He did not like including civilians in a war. If the small square in front of him was soon to become a battleground, it was no place for innocent bystanders.

Carter tensed.

From the hills to his right an old, long-bed pickup with high stake sides wheezed around a sloping curve and made its way up the dusty main street.

Just short of the bar it turned left and rumbled its nose into an alley, leaving half the bed sticking into the street. The truck was crated high with fresh produce.

The driver, a swarthy youth of about twenty with long black hair and a sorry excuse for a Pancho Villa mustache, slid from the cab. He moved to the truck's rear and, after lowering the tailgate, began stacking crates of produce on it.

Market day? To take advantage of the crowd coming to hear Mendez speak?

Maybe. Maybe not.

Carter relaxed back in his chair, but he kept the driver and the truck in his peripheral vision.

The church bell began a steady hollow clang from its hillside steeple.

The pupils of Carter's gray eyes played pendulum up and down the street.

Would the villagers do as they had been told?

Had all of them gotten the word?

Evidently so.

Nothing moved in the heat-hazed air.

Except the driver of the pickup loaded with produce. He was probably a truck farmer from somewhere deep back in the hills. He would not have gotten the word.

Should Carter tell him?

He was about to push himself out of the chair, when the driver stepped onto the porch and headed his way.

He wore faded and worn blue jeans, a plaid shirt, its tail out and flapping, and a white, wide-brimmed straw hat.

His feet made an odd, thumping sound on the porch boards. Carter saw why. He wore huaraches—woven leather sandals with the soles fashioned from old rubber tire casings.

He was halfway to the door when he stopped, eying Carter.

"Buenos dias."

"Buenos dias," came the reply.

He removed his hat in the peasant manner, reaching behind his head and lifting it from the rear. By so doing, it covered his face for a moment as a sign of respect. Then he dropped the straw to waist level. This was also a sign of respect, as well as showing that he was unarmed.

"Americano?"

"Sí," Carter replied, feeling the familiar itch of caution crawl up his spine as the man rattled off several sentences of garbled Spanish that Carter did not completely understand.

Something was wrong, but Carter could not put his finger on it.

"No comprendo."

The man shrugged. He made a single step toward the bar door and paused again.

"Uno cigarrillo . . . por favor?"

Carter pulled a pack from his pocket with his left hand and shook one out.

"Gracias, señor."

Carter nodded and watched the back of the plaid shirt retreat into the bar.

The man looked like a peasant, but something about him was wrong. He had spoken Spanish, not Basque, and yet his Spanish had been oddly accented.

And there was something else, something different that didn't fit.

Before Carter could finger it, the sudden backfire of a car returned his attention to the street. A bent-fendered, barely running 1950 Ford, its black paint gray with dust, lurched and bolted toward the square.

The church bell seemed to peal louder the closer the old car came. This drew Carter's eye for a brief second.

What he saw sent a quick whispered curse from his lips.

A line of eight monks, all in traditional long brown robes,

was moving down the hill from the monastery. They trudged, single file, their heads bent, their hands folded over their bellies, directly toward the square.

Damnit, Carter thought. Hubanyo had screwed up. The monks on the hill had not been told!

He sat upright in the chair as the old Ford reached the edge of the square and rattled to a halt. The two deputies who had been lounging against the speaker's platform moved toward it. At the same time, the huge, potbellied bulk of Hubanyo himself emerged from one of the false-fronted stores on the other side of the Ford. He toted a shotgun cradled in his fat arms, and his black eyes leaped up and down the empty streets.

But he did not see the monks descending the hill behind him.

The bottom half of Carter's right trouser leg had been split and then Velcroed together for easy access to his ever faithful Luger, Wilhelmina. As the two rear doors of the Ford opened, he slid a finger into the Velcro at the top of the slit.

A tall, reed-thin man with angular features and receding gray hair unwound from the back of the sedan on Hubanyo's side.

A small, uniformed man with sleepy eyes and lethargic movements stepped from the Ford on Carter's side.

Carter mentally cursed.

This sorry excuse for a soldier was obviously the body-guard Madrid had provided Mendez. He looked like a left-over from Franco's era and, as such, probably hated Julio Mendez and everything the man stood for, then and now.

The driver was pushing seventy, also no help. He was already leaning his head back against the seat as if he were headed directly for siesta.

The two deputies had reached Mendez's "bodyguard." Hubanyo was talking to Mendez, gesturing toward the small building behind him and shaking his head from side to side.

If it was going down, it would be soon now.

There was a tiny ripping sound as Carter's finger began opening the Velcro.

Call it *déjà vu* or call it the sixth sense of the trained operative, the survival instinct that had kept Killmaster N3 alive through many missions.

Or call it the reality of what was: a slight rocking of the old pickup, the monks shifting from single file to fan out in their movement.

And the thump of a rubber-soled footstep on the porch behind him.

The driver.

Carter was no language expert, but he knew a little of the local dialect, and Cubanez had taught him more in their short time together.

The driver had definitely spoken Spanish, but it suddenly hit Carter that it was neither the local dialect nor even decent peasant Spanish.

It was Mexican Spanish.

And then he remembered the huaraches . . . Mexican peasant shoes.

If a Mexican wanted comfortable footwear to do a big job, he might very well wear what he was most accustomed to. . . .

Carter ripped the Velcro all the way and filled his hand with the Luger. At the same time, he lurched to the right, out of the chair, and rolled in the air.

The young driver, a toothy grin spreading his mahogany face, stood in the bar's doorway. His arms were straight out from his body, his hand holding an already barking .357.

The magnum's slugs made kindling out of the chair back Carter had just vacated.

Carter's back hit the porch just as Wilhelmina exploded. It

threw his aim off slightly, but it was still a hit.

The slug thudded into the guy's left hip bone, spinning him around. He hit the wall belly first, staining a good chunk of the faded whitewash with his gore before turning again for a second try at the rolling figure.

Carter squeezed off two rounds: one dead center into the guy's gut, the other a head shot.

The magnum flew from his hands as if on invisible strings, and he was flattened against the wall. He was faceless and his belly was belching blood.

Carter rolled to his belly on the porch, the Luger in his outstretched hands.

All hell had busted loose around him.

Three gunmen had erupted from the bed of the pickup. They all held barking semiautomatic rifles. Their fire was witheringly directed at Hubanyo and Mendez, but most of it was doing nothing more than making scrap out of the Ford.

Carter took in all the rest of the dusty scene in a split second.

The eight monks were each on one knee. From beneath their robes they had produced everything from Brownings to .357s.

Hubanyo had wrestled Mendez three-quarters of the way to the buildings, so they were out of the monks' line of fire.

The two deputies and the bodyguard had not been so lucky.

The uniformed man lay next to the Ford, his body cut nearly in half. One of the two deputies had made it back to the speaker's platform, where he now lay throwing a little fire—when he could raise his head—toward the pickup. The other deputy had been hit in the right leg and was under the Ford, partially shielded by the front wheels.

He wouldn't last long, Carter thought.

It had all happened fast. Maybe ten seconds. And it was happening faster.

Cubanez had already opened up on the monks, dropping two of them with fast fire from the Galil. The others were hustling to positions behind the stores and nearby rocks.

The three in the rear of the pickup had been so intent on trying to nail Mendez that they had not noticed that their buddy had failed to waste the *Americano* on the porch.

Carter dived through the door of the bar and scuttled across the large room. Near the rear he found a window. When it would not open, he kicked it out, frame and all, with his booted foot.

He dived through, headfirst. Hitting the dust with his shoulder, he rolled and came up on his feet like a cat, the Luger ready to blow hell out of whomever its dark, deadly snout could find.

Through the windshield and the rear window of the truck, he could see them. All three were still intent on the square.

Carter was halfway to the truck when one of them rolled over the bed and headed for the cab.

His intent was obvious; he would move the pickup out and make it a rolling tank.

He saw Carter just as he stepped on the running board. He was toting an M-16, but he saw his executioner too late to bring it into play.

In mid-stride Carter pumped two from the Luger into his chest. Cloth ripped, blood spread, and the slugs exited, fanning the air behind with flesh.

He had barely toppled out of sight when Carter leaped up onto the hood. His belly hit, and his legs curled. The heavily ridged soles of his boots caught, and he was lying belly-out across the roof.

He fanned Wilhelmina from left to right, sending 9mm steel jackets into the backs of their skulls.

One quick eyeball gave him the situation.

Fire was still coming from behind the rocks to the side of

the stores. The monks there could not fire into the front doors and windows, but they could keep anybody inside from coming out.

Cubanez was doing a good job of keeping them pinned down with his Model 12.

Firing from the rear of the stores told Carter that the rest of the monks were around there, probably massing for an assault on the rear door.

The two men he had just sent to hell had been firing an Enfield and an old Garand.

Leathering the Luger, he jackknifed off the roof and slid into the cab.

The old engine coughed and sputtered a couple of times but finally caught. When Carter was sure it was running—and would stay that way—he floored it and jammed the shift into first.

The alley was narrow. So much so that, deeper in, the fenders scraped the sides of adobe huts. Steel screamed against hard-packed mud, but Carter did not let up.

He shifted, closed his ears to the engine's screams of protest, and burst into the open at the rear of the bar.

Two hard rights brought him to another alley that led him back to the front of the bar and the square.

Again the alley was too narrow. A fender let go with a piercing shriek of metal and flew over the top of the cab.

The nose of the old truck had barely cleared the front of the alley when slugs from behind the rocks stitched the windshield.

Shattered glass sprayed across Carter's chest and shoulders but did little harm. He was already lying prone across the seat, one foot to the floor, one hand driving toward the jeep from memory.

When he was sure he had cleared the other vehicle by at least a few feet, he cranked the truck around, lifted his foot from the accelerator, and stomped the brake with both feet.

Tricky? Yes, but he had walked the ground for hours that morning and figured he could gauge the distance from memory.

The old pickup teetered on its nose and then two wheels. Just as it started to go over, Carter gave it up.

He slithered, belly down, out the passenger side. His right hand partially broke his fall just before he tucked, rolled, and came up in a crouch.

Not perfect, but close.

The truck, now on its side, upper wheels still spinning crazily, blocked all of the jeep except a bit of its rear end.

But he would have to hurry. The monks behind the rocks were zeroing in, obviously reading his plans and trying for the jeep's tires.

Once in the seat, Carter unearthed the Model 12 and fired up the engine.

"*Amigo . . . !*"

Cubanez's voice reached him through the sound of gunfire from across the street. He was partially leaning out a side window, away from the slugs coming from behind the rocks.

"Did Hubanyo and Mendez make it?" Carter shouted.

"Affirmative! They are in the hardware store . . . it is the one in the center!"

Carter nodded. "How many left?"

"Near as I can tell, five. Two behind those rocks, three behind the store."

"Cover me!"

Cubanez gave a thumbs-up sign and disappeared.

Carter roared back down the alley he had just come up with the truck. Once through, he cranked left and gave the little machine all it could take. He went on by the alley where the truck had been originally parked and kept turning.

Soon he was beyond the village shacks and bouncing

crazily over open country. When he was a good thousand yards from the village, he banked left and began to climb.

Rocks, ruts, and generally rough terrain gave the jeep hell, but eventually Carter came out on the road that led back into the village.

He 180'd the jeep and skidded to a halt on the far side of the curve, out of sight from below.

From a webbed pouch between the seats, he chose three M-34 incendiary grenades and arranged them in the passenger seat. With a new magazine in Wilhelmina, who was back in his leg holster, Carter looked to the Model 12.

He fixed the stock and draped the lanyard over his left shoulder. When he dropped the jeep's windshield, the space between the left-hand grip and the magazine fitted perfectly down over the round bar at the base of the windshield.

It would serve as a reverse bi-pod of the sub, allowing Carter to fire, release the Beretta without it flopping, and throw the grenades, only to regrip and fire again.

He was ready.

Carter went through the gears quickly, hitting fifty by the time he rounded the curve.

The chatter of renewed gunfire found his ears as the jeep's nose dipped and he hurtled downward, directly for the dusty square and the area toward the storefront beyond it.

At one hundred yards he started firing. The little Model 12 bucked in his hand but stayed in place on the windshield bar.

The monks had shed their robes. Beneath them they wore green and brown fatigues. Carter could see insignia, and he guessed it matched that worn by the dead "bodyguard" near the Ford.

That would be their game.

Carter could almost see the headlines: "Government Troops Kill Leftist Leader."

At fifty yards he let up on the accelerator and released the Beretta.

There had been some confusion behind the rocks when the two shooters had seen that they were flanked and still being fired upon from the bar.

But they quickly recovered.

Now one had shifted around to return Carter's fire while the other still concentrated on Cubanez. But between the peppering fire from the two angles, neither of them could get off a shot that would do any damage.

Carter released the Beretta and, in three-second intervals, threw the grenades. The M-34 had about a five-second fuse. By the time the first one went off, Carter was firing again.

The first grenade was short.

The second wasn't.

The body that had been firing at Cubanez lifted into the air and settled down over a boulder, arms and legs sprawled grotesquely in every direction.

Just as the jeep reached the narrowed lane leading up to the monastery, the third blast rocked the air.

Carter's shooter stood. He dropped his weapon and staggered from behind the rocks, his hands vainly tearing at his ripped and scorched eyes.

Carter made the turn, lifting the muzzle of the Model 12 around and laying it across his right arm.

The guy was fifteen yards from the jeep when he started crying out in Spanish: "I'm finished . . . I'm finished!"

"You bet your ass you are," Carter hissed, and laid a burst across his chest from nipple to nipple.

At the top of the hill, Carter slid lithely from the jeep. Ejecting the nearly empty magazine, he jacked in a fresh one and started down the incline a boulder at a time.

From far across the square, Cubanez and his Beretta were

quiet. Carter could not see the head of one or the muzzle of the other above the window casing.

Good man.

Cubanez was already moving out, probably far to the right and below Carter to give him backing if he needed it.

Halfway to the bottom, Carter stopped.

Firing was intermittent now.

A pop or two from just beneath him would bring small-arms fire from the second floor rear of the hardware store.

Carter waited until he could get a fix, then moved out again.

He placed two of them, one in some rocks right at the base of the hill. The other was just below his present position, on a direct line with the second-story window.

Where was number three?

Carter found out all too soon.

A tiny scrape. Boot sole against stone.

He whirled, the Model 12 bucking in both hands.

The guy got off one shot. Carter felt the sting and tug of the slug at his left ear as his own slugs tore into the guy's gut.

He screamed. Once. And then toppled backward over the rocks to lay silent.

Carter didn't wait now. He moved on down through the rocky killing ground, his ears attuned to every sound.

Alerted by the burping fire of the Model 12 above them, the two remaining shooters had slipped their positions.

"*Señor* Carter . . ."

Carter looked up.

Hubanyo's fat, florid face was in the window.

"To your right—behind the two trees!"

Carter moved right in a crouch. He took his sight lines off the tops of two scrub oaks that angled toward the sky from above the line of rocks.

Every five feet he stopped to listen.

Nothing.

And then he heard it: the soft pad of booted feet on dry dirt.

The guy had flanked him. He was moving up now through the rocks to Carter's right, about twenty yards in the rear.

Carter smiled to himself. He hunkered down and waited, filling his hand with a good-sized rock.

It wasn't long.

When the guy was directly on the other side of Carter's boulder, he rolled the rock over the top.

The firing was instantaneous.

That was the way Carter found him when he came around, rifle in the air, firing at sound.

Carter centered the death end of the Beretta on his chest and planted his feet.

"You can live, *amigo.*"

The guy cursed loudly and brought his rifle down in an arc, firing.

The man screamed in agony when the first 9mm slug hit his shoulder.

The screaming ended in a gurgling death rattle when the next four took his head off.

The sound of the Model 12 had barely died out when Carter heard Cubanez's voice calling to him from near the edge of the buildings.

"*Amigo* . . . Nick!"

"Yeah?"

"How many did you get?"

"Two behind the rocks and two up here."

"Then it is over. We are coming out."

We? Carter thought, moving cautiously the rest of the way down the hill, still in cover.

He hit the bottom just as Cubanez came around the side of

the building. The Spaniard had a wide grin on his face, and the muzzle of his Beretta ground into the soft spot behind a man's ear.

"His name is Manuel Ortiz," Cubanez said. "He is Cuban and, as you Americans would say, he is scared shitless."

Carter smiled.

They had their prisoner.

FOUR

Nick Carter sighed in contentment as the strong yet wondrously gentle and feminine hands floated down over his bare back. They moved like feathers over his naked buttocks, then slid between his legs.

The fingers did amazing things, until the pleasure threatened to turn into pain.

"You like?" asked the sultry voice.

"I love," Carter replied and rolled over onto his back.

She was gorgeous, all five-foot-ten of her, full of pleasurable angles and even more pleasurable curves. Her breasts were bare, as was the rest of her, and they hung like two huge melons directly above Carter's eyes.

Her name was Delores, and Carter had met her on the flight back from Madrid three days before.

The attraction had been instantaneous and mutual.

"What do you do?" she had asked.

"I'm a reporter for Amalgamated Press and Wire Services," Carter had replied without blinking. "I'm just getting off an assignment in Spain. And you?"

"I'm rich."

"Oh?"

"Yeah. I like to read, gamble, play tennis, travel, and make love . . . not necessarily in that order."

Her eyes had said the rest.

"I have to file my story when we land. It should take about two hours. Can I meet you for dinner?"

"Sure." She scribbled her address. It was near Carter's apartment in Arlington. "I'll have something brought in."

"You don't have to."

"I want to. By the time you get to my place you may not be hungry . . . for food, I mean."

Carter wasn't sure she was legit, but with that face, that figure, and all that blond hair, he wanted to find out.

It should have taken him two hours to file the Spanish report. He did it in just fifty minutes and took another ten briefing Hawk.

The prisoner confirmed just about everything. Nels Pomroy was indeed the go-between. Whoever the head of the far left wing of ETA was, he wanted Julio Mendez out of the way. Pomroy had hired a freelance shooter originally, but the guy had obviously failed or balked on the contract at the last minute.

When the arms unexpectedly fell into Pomroy's hands, he hatched the plan to trade off with the Latinos for Freedom.

The prisoner they had captured had so spilled his guts that his buddies in Mexico and Belize would be under surveillance within twenty-four hours. At the first sign of any more activity, they could all be picked up by the local police or security organization.

All nice and neatly wrapped up.

"Maybe," Hawk said. "And maybe not."

"But that's about as much as I can do," Carter said.

Hawk nodded. "Take a week. Relax, but stay in touch."

"Will do," Carter replied, and ten minutes later he was giving a cabbie Delores Teller's address in Arlington.

She met him in a sheer negligée that didn't hide a wispy pair of panties and a bra that couldn't begin to contain the occupants of its cups.

"Hungry?"

"Yeah.."

"Food?"

"No."

"The bedroom's this way."

That had been three days before. They had eaten several meals, but as yet they had never put their clothes back on.

Among the other delightful things Delores did, she gave massages. About the time Carter figured he was going down for the last time, Delores gave him a massage.

It never failed.

"What are you looking at?"

"The bottom of your breasts. They're amazing."

"Why?"

"They don't sag."

"I do exercises. Want to go to Monte Carlo?"

That was another odd little twist to her personality. She often changed the subject in mid-sentence, and it was always interesting to Carter to hear the new thought she came up with.

"Why Monte Carlo?"

She shrugged. "I dunno. I think you'd be a ball to be with in Monte Carlo. We could read, travel, gamble, play tennis . . ."

"And make love all at the same time." Carter grinned.

"Yeah. Want to?"

"Can't right now, Delores. But we can make love."

"All right."

That was something else Carter liked about Delores. She was a very agreeable lady.

She leaned forward until her breasts grazed his face.

"Kiss them, Nick, honey. Make them hurt with your kisses the way you did before."

Her breasts were milky white and the nipples were darker than pink, almost crimson in the dim light.

But it wasn't the color as much as the touch.

Carter reached with both hands and caressed the smooth flesh. The nipples seemed to harden at his touch, and she forced them one by one to his lips.

His eyes rolled upward to hers. They were green, widely set in her beautiful face, and right now they were flashing with an animal sensuality that told Carter she did not want to wait much longer.

"Delores, you amaze me. Lie down."

Her laugh was genuine, coming spontaneously from the long, clean line of her throat. And it was no little-girl giggle; it was the throaty chuckle of an amused woman.

"Why? Because it's only six o'clock in the morning?" she said, sliding into the bed beside him.

"That's one reason," Carter said, burying his face in her blond mane and rolling his hips between her thighs. "But there are about a million more."

Their bodies collided, and they were instantly in the throes of a lusty rhythm. Her breaths and sighs, her clutching hands and her heels hitting his buttocks were all spurs, making Carter pound into her body with a force that he thought had left him long ago.

"Good, so good," she growled, biting his lip even while kissing it.

"Only because you are so wild," he replied.

At last her passion peaked. It drew a scream from her lips and an arch from her body that brought Carter to his own climax.

At first he thought it was some new, strange sound coming from Delores. By now he had learned that during—and even after—lovemaking, the woman could indeed come up with strange sounds.

And then he realized that it was the beeper.

"No . . . where . . . ?" she groaned, feeling him slide out of her.

"Have to . . . telephone," he replied, padding across the room.

"Nick . . ."

"Sorry." He dialed, and even at six A.M. there was only one ring.

"Amalgamated."

"Extension two hundred."

The mechanical gnomes made clicks on the line, and Ginger Bateman's husky rasp filled his ear.

"Two hundred."

"It's me."

"Come . . . pronto."

"Oh, Christ . . ."

"Here, Nick. Now!"

"It's six o'clock in the morning."

"You think I don't know that? I slept here last night. P-R-O-N-T-O!"

"Your Spanish is lousy," Carter hissed, but she had already hung up.

"What the hell are you doing?"

Delores was sitting up in bed, her breasts a huge, tantalizing shelf over her folded arms. Anger and rejection were already starting to form in the green pools of her eyes.

"I have to go into the office for a while."

"You don't . . ."

"I do."

She practically broke the bed when she fell back on it.

"Damn all you people who work for a living. When will you be back?"

"As soon as I can. I promise."

"You mean it?"

"I mean it."

"I hope so," she said, sitting up again. "There's something about you that's . . . well, nice."

"You, too," Carter said and kissed the tip of her nose. At the door he paused and turned. "Delores . . . ?"

"Yeah?"

"If I don't get right back . . . I mean . . . well, how about leaving word with your service where you'll be?"

"Then it might be a while?"

"It might," he admitted.

"Hey."

"Yeah?"

He turned. She was smiling and her eyes said, "It's me again."

"Yeah. Just check my service."

It was torture all the way to Dupont Circle not to remember how she looked, naked, sitting in that bed.

It was one half hour later to the minute when Carter arrived at the Amalgamated Press and Wire Services Offices. Amalgamated put out a couple of magazines a month and ran a small news service. But it was all a front for AXE and allowed the ultrasecret agency to have field offices all over the world under the guise of "news gathering services."

Out of these field offices operated the men with "N" designations. Nick Carter was one of them: "N3, Killmaster." There had once been N1 and N2, but they had long since bought the farm.

Agent N3, Nick Carter, was top dog among the field agents.

But that meant nothing when David Hawk said "Jump!"

Or, in this case, "Pronto!"

Carter was through final security within two minutes of his initial arrival and at Hawk's office thirty seconds after that.

"He's waiting."

Ginger Bateman sat behind her desk, partially hidden by a mountain of papers. Normally she was the most perfect composite of brains and beauty the Good Lord could fashion from a hank of hair and a hunk of bone.

Now she was a mess.

Her sable hair with its brilliant deep-red highlights was in total disarray, and there were lines around her eyes and mouth that did not agree at all with her perfect features.

"I thought all was calm."

"All was calm, but all of a sudden all is chaos. The big man has had us all running all night like there was no tomorrow."

"You look like hell."

"Thank you, Nick. We've been going for two days, twenty-four hours a day, nonstop."

"What's up?"

"The missile heist in Germany a few months ago. Remember it?"

"I read the bulletins."

"Good, then you're briefed. Go on in."

She dropped her head into her hands and began massaging her temples with the tips of her fingers. For the moment Carter forgot Delores.

"Hey . . ."

"What?"

"Dinner tonight?"

"Impossible," she said with a chuckle.

"Why?"

"You'll be in Paris."

"Then we'll dine at Maxim's."

The beautiful features cast off their weariness for a second, and her lips spread in a wide smile.

"You're incorrigible—"

"And in love, and hungry, and horn—"

"Scram . . . before he swallows his cigar."

She buzzed him through the massive oak doors, and Carter entered the walnut-walled inner sanctum.

The air conditioner hummed at full throttle, but it was fighting a losing battle with the brown rope wedged in the corner of David Hawk's mouth.

"Carter. Good, sit! Drink?"

"No, thank you, sir. It's a little early for me." He coughed, twice, and lowered himself into a huge leather antique. The chair was so soft that Carter could barely see the other man over the piled top of the huge mahogany desk.

"Good. You familiar with this?"

A stapled file folder flew across the desk and landed on Carter's lap.

"Yes, sir. I've kept up with the bulletins."

"Well, as of this morning they're outdated. We think we might have a link between the missiles and the disappearance of two men: Adam Greenspan and Lorenzo Montegra."

"Who are they?"

Two more folders found their way into Carter's hands. Instead of case files, these were dossiers.

"Look them over, N3, all of them, carefully," Hawk rasped. "And think about our recent soiree in northern Spain while you're at it. I'll get us some coffee."

Carter lit a cigarette, thought of Delores, thought of Ginger Bateman, and opened the first folder.

It was titled: MISSILE THEFT—EUROPE—TOP SE-CRET. . . .

It had all begun on a clear but moonless night six months earlier, outside Enschede, near the Netherlands-West German frontier.

Because of increasing peace marches that had nearly developed into riots in The Hague and Rotterdam, NATO Command in Belgium had decided to remove eight medium-range missiles from the Netherlands.

It was not an earth-shaking decision. The missiles were practically obsolete and would have been replaced or removed soon anyway.

They were moved across the West German border in a caravan consisting of two sixteen-wheeler semi transports, a staff officer's car, and two armored personnel carriers.

In addition to heavy ordnance in the personnel carriers, four men armed with heavy-caliber machine guns rode on the top of each trailer.

From the standpoint of hardware, the caravan could have held off a small army.

Their destination was a NATO-leased factory outside Hamburg. Once there, the missiles would be broken down into components, deactivated, and sent on to Frankfurt in separate shipments. From Frankfurt they would be flown back to the United States and either destroyed or stored.

They never reached Hamburg.

Outside Bremen, the caravan entered a long tunnel. Just before the far end of the tunnel, a large section of the roadway had been dynamited, making it impassable. Over the end of the tunnel, a huge polyethylene tent had been secured.

The officer in charge, sensing an attack on his cargo, ordered his men to the rear of the caravan. There, guns primed, they began to lead the vehicles back out the end of the tunnel they had just entered.

They never made it.

Another charge had been set at that end of the tunnel, as well as another airtight polyethylene cover.

Through the vents in the roof of the tunnel, a deadly gas was pumped into the semidarkness by a powerful generator.

Chaos reigned supreme in this sudden gas chamber, but it

only lasted a few minutes.

They died to a man.

Runners were placed across the blown-out portion of the roadway, and the trucks continued on their journey . . . only now in the hands of hijackers.

From the time the missiles left the tunnel, it was all speculation bolstered by the accounts of a few witnesses.

Their final destination inside Germany was evidently the northern port of Bremerhaven.

That same night, a Libyan-registered freighter sailed from Bremerhaven. She was the *Star of Ceylon*, and her first port of call was Malta.

She never arrived.

Rounding the tip of Portugal, thirty miles out and still some distance from Gibraltar, the *Star of Ceylon* radioed a mayday. There had been a massive internal explosion in the bowels of the ship. Fire had already spread from bow to stern.

By the time Portuguese and Spanish air-sea rescue units had arrived, the *Star of Ceylon* had sunk with all hands.

The lines between NATO headquarters and Brussels went wild. The Mediterranean fleet attempted exploratory dives, all to no avail.

The question hung like a leaden cloud over all concerned. . . .

Had the eight obsolete but still deadly missiles gone down with the ill-fated *Star of Ceylon?*

Or had the missiles been off-loaded from the freighter before her "accident" had taken place?

Carter closed the folder and dropped it on Hawk's desk. He rubbed the room's smoke from his eyes and heard a cup rattle against a saucer at his elbow.

"Cream or sugar?"

"Black," Carter replied.

"Finished?"

"Just the missile file. Not much I didn't already know, except the supposition about current whereabouts."

"Read the dossiers," Hawk replied, "and I'll fill you in."

Carter opened the first folder and read quickly.

Two weeks after the missiles' theft, Adam Greenspan, architect, arrived in Milan, Italy.

His intent was a few weeks of skiing at the Rapiti resort in the Dolomites near Bolzano.

After renting a Mercedes at the Milan airport, Greenspan supposedly drove north toward Bolzano.

He never arrived.

There was only one clue to his disappearance. Before leaving Milan, he had made one stop at the Hotel Excelsior Gallia to meet a woman. The doorman remembered putting the woman's bags into the trunk of the Mercedes.

The doorman usually remembered Mercedes. They went along with large tips. Adam Greenspan was no different. He had tipped the doorman ten thousand lire.

The woman had been registered at the Excelsior under the name of Carmen D'Angelo.

Normally, the disappearance of an American architect would not raise very many eyebrows. The disappearance of Adam Greenspan did.

Reason?

He was a genius in his field, one of the few experienced designers of concrete launching pads and storage silos for ballistic missiles.

Carter looked up from the Greenspan folder and whistled.

"That's only part of it," Hawk said. "Go on."

Carter took a sip of the coffee, chain-lit yet another cigarette, and opened the folder with MONTEGRA written across its top right-hand corner.

Lorenzo Montegra was a first generation Mexican-American from San Diego, California. His coworkers at Hughes Aircraft in L.A. disliked Montegra, but they admired his brains and skill.

Why the dislike?

Because Lorenzo Montegra had it all. At Stanford University, he had been one of the highest-ranking amateur tennis players in the world, as well as a Phi Beta Kappa in physics and math.

As an independent consultant to Hughes on systems and radar, he had made a small fortune.

And Montegra enjoyed his wealth. He had movie-star good looks and the athletic physique to go with it.

Women—even the wives of his coworkers—had a soft spot in their hearts for Lorenzo.

And he for them.

Two months after the theft of the missiles in West Germany, Montegra was seen almost constantly in the company of a woman from Olivera Street in downtown Los Angeles.

Her name was Maria Estrada, and no one was surprised when Montegra announced that he was spending his entire vacation at the woman's villa outside Ensenada, Mexico.

Indeed, they all sighed with relief. Maria Estrada was perfect for Montegra. She was darkly beautiful, as only Latin women are. She had breasts, hips, and thighs that would make the mouth of a corpse water. And she obviously had money: a home in Los Angeles and a villa in Ensenada.

Maria Estrada fit Lorenzo Montegra to a T.

Perhaps they would marry, and then all the married men who moved in Montegra's circle could breathe easier.

But it didn't happen that way.

Four days after their arrival in Ensenada, the couple went deep-sea fishing. They, two deckhands, and the fishing boat's skipper were all lost in a freak storm.

The storm was a freak because it came up with no warning,

not because it was a killer. It was no more than a light squall. Four other fishing boats had been out in it at the time, and all four of them had reached port easily and safely.

Carter tossed both folders on the desk and lifted the cup and saucer with hands that were now shaking visibly.

"What do you think?" Hawk asked through what had now become a heavy pall of blue-gray smoke between them.

"Heavy. If there is a connection, the missiles are alive and well, and somebody plans on mounting and firing them."

"It looks that way," Hawk said, nodding. He mashed the mangled remnants of his cigar, then immediately clipped and lit another. "Of course, if we green light an agent to go into the field and do something about this, we must assume that the missiles are not in a freighter's hull sitting on the bottom of the ocean."

Hawk rarely smiled. Now he was grinning like a cat about to make an easy kill.

"I take it," Carter said, "that we now have something that allows us to make that assumption?"

"You take it right, Nick, thanks to the Yucatán-Spain-Basque connection."

"What?"

If anything, the grin widened. Hard to do around a cigar, but Hawk managed it. His hamlike hands found yet another set of papers before he spoke again.

"Balikin Arms Limited of Amsterdam shipped— legally—a large consignment of light and heavy mortars, machine guns, automatic rifles, handguns, and ammunition out of Germany with an end-use certificate for Malta."

The hair stood up on the back of Carter's neck, and his knuckles gleamed white as his fingers gripped the coffee cup.

"The *Star of Ceylon*," he whispered.

"Neat as a pin," Hawk replied.

"I'll be damned."

"I don't think it's too much to assume that, if they off-loaded a shipment of arms for use as barter material in a kill, they would overlook eight missiles.''

Here Hawk leaned back and diligently applied a desk lighter to the end of his cigar. By the time it was boiling smoke, the smile on his broad face had been replaced by a studied frown.

''When all this began to dovetail so neatly, we dug back into the Greenspan and Montegra disappearances. It didn't take a genius or a computer to see how they fit.''

''How was the connection made?'' Carter asked, lighting a cigarette himself in self-defense.

''A woman.'' Hawk searched the mess on his desk for a moment, found what he wanted, and then continued. ''We've pretty well established that the woman in Milan at the Excelsior Gallia—'Carmen D'Angelo'—and 'Maria Estrada' in Los Angeles were one and the same.''

''That's a little too much coincidence.''

''You're damned right it is! We would have been stymied at that, however, if we hadn't dug a little further into Adam Greenspan's life.''

''And . . . ?'' Carter sat up a little straighter in his chair now.

The missile theft was big, but for all intents and purposes, the military could take care of its own problems. If the problem had been passed along to AXE, with the kind of operatives the agency used and their methods of solution, then it had gotten even bigger and more dangerous.

''A little over a year ago, Adam Greenspan finished overseeing the installation of six silos at a secret base in West Germany. He took a three-week vacation skiing in Gstaad, Switzerland. While he was there he met a woman named Armanda de Nerro.''

Carter screwed his face into a frown of concentration. As fast as possible, he went through the computerlike memory bank of names in his mind, but he came up blank.

Hawk caught it and smiled.

"You wouldn't know the lady, Carter. In our line of work we rarely travel in her set. Anyway, we did a rundown, got some pictures, and did one hell of a lot of legwork."

"All three women are one and the same," Carter growled.

Hawk nodded. "Doorman and concierge in Milan nailed her straight. Italians don't forget beautiful women, particularly when they go along with big tips. A realtor in L.A. remembers renting the house to her as Maria Estrada, and a maid in Ensenada definitely identified de Nerro's photograph as her mistress at the villa that Estrada rented down there."

"Any way to tie her to Nels Pomroy as well?"

"Only by a roundabout connection through a Basque terrorist, Lupe de Varga. Her file can fill you in there later. De Varga had several connections with Pomroy . . . we think. Just how much came out of them, we don't know yet, but we're digging. In the meantime, the woman is the only real lead and/or link we have."

"And right now Armanda de Nerro is in Paris."

"No. How did you come up with that?"

"Bateman said I would be having dinner in Paris."

"You will, but not to meet de Nerro. What do you know about Andorra?"

Again Carter's mind switched into high gear, this time coming up with a winner.

"It's a principality nestled in the Pyrenees Mountains between Spain and France. It's small, about one hundred and eighty square miles. It's become known as the world's discount shopping center because of its lack of taxes and tariffs, and, lately, it's skyrocketed in popularity with the world's tax evaders."

"That's enough for now," Hawk said. "We've leased a villa for you in Andorra from a wealthy expatriate Englishman. Ever hear of Nicholas Carstocus?''

"No,'' Carter replied.

"You wouldn't have. He always operated very quietly under the international code name 'Bluebeard.' ''

"Bluebeard I've heard of,'' Carter said, his mental antennae now on full alert.

In one way or another, Bluebeard had been involved with fifteen or more high-level assassinations in the last ten years. He was a master craftsman, and no one had been able to get a line on what he looked like or his identity.

Carter said as much to Hawk.

"Not until about three months ago. The French secret service, SDECE, not only got a line on him, they uncovered him.''

Hawk did a quick scan of some notes on a paper before him then spoke again.

"Carstocus was the son of Greek immigrants. He was born in New York and, as a child, had every advantage. His family clan were very wealthy restaurateurs. When the father passed away, young Nicholas took over the family business, and he prospered. When his mother died, he sold the business and started making the jet-set scene as an international playboy, but he kept a fairly low profile.''

"But the French put something together?''

"Right,'' Hawk said, nodding. "About two years ago Carstocus moved to Paris, and Bluebeard's operations stepped up. A couple of months ago, the SDECE got enough proof to nail him.''

"Where is he now?''

"Dead. He was very quietly killed while resisting arrest and now resides in an unmarked grave outside Paris.''

"And I'm to take his place,'' Carter said. "Did he have anything to do with the stolen missiles?''

"Nothing. Evidently assassinations—the planning and

execution of them—was all Carstocus cared about. It was his idea of success, proving to himself that he was just a little bit better than anyone else in the world. The money was secondary.''

"Nice guy," Carter drawled.

"Paris SDECE has agreed to set you up with everything they have on Carstocus. From Paris you take off for Andorra.''

"Why Andorra?"

"Two reasons. The first is just theory, a wild guess. Andorra is at the opposite end of the Pyrenees from Basque country, around San Sebastian. Spanish Guardia Civil do not cross the border into Andorra.''

Carter nodded. "So if the Basques were behind the missile heist and they are moving them into Andorra . . .''

"Exactly. The second reason you're going to Andorra is because Armanda de Nerro lives there.''

Two more thick files were passed across the desk to Carter.

"One," Hawk said, "is the life of Armanda de Nerro. It makes interesting reading. The other is a background file on the ETA—the Euzkadi Ta Askatasuna.''

"The Basque terrorist network," Carter said, hefting both of the files at once.

Hawk nodded. "That will be your homework on the flight from Dulles. You leave in two hours.''

Carter checked his watch and frowned. "The last commercial flight has already left for Paris . . .''

"You're not flying commercial. The Vice-President is meeting day after tomorrow with the heads of the Common Market countries in Paris. I've managed to sneak you aboard Air Force Two as an Amalgamated reporter. Disappear right after you land at Orly, and check in with SDECE as soon as possible.''

A last question popped into Carter's mind as Hawk stood.

"Why Carstocus?"

"Because of his trade," Hawk barked, softening it with a lopsided grin. "We're going to leak the fact that Nicholas Carstocus is Bluebeard. That should make nice bait, don't you think?"

FIVE

Nick Carter managed to lose himself with the elite of the press corps on Air Force Two.

When the plane was airborne and he was fortified with three fingers of expensive scotch, he gravitated away from the others and found a solo seat.

Then he started on the files, beginning with Armanda de Nerro.

She was quite a lady.

The de Nerro clan was Basque to the core. They were wealthy landowners, and their presence in the Basque state of Navarra near Pamplona went back years.

Armanda's grandfather, Don Pepe de Nerro, had fought with all his heart on the Loyalist side against Franco. Later, when the Fascist dictatorship became firmly entrenched in power, his son Luis carried on the fight as the leader of an underground guerrilla organization.

Eventually, Luis was unmasked. His lands were confiscated, and he fled to France and exile, taking the now aging Don Pepe with him.

That was in 1951, the same year Luis's daughter, Armanda, was born in Carcassonne, France.

Though his lands had been lost, Luis had managed to flee

61

with enough money to retain his life-style in exile and carry on his fight against Franco.

The fact that he had married the daughter of another wealthy Basque exile, Don Ramon de Leon, also did not hurt his financial position.

Luis's wife, Maria, was as rabidly anti-France and pro-Basque as her husband, but there was no record of her becoming a guerrilla fighter like Luis.

Quite the opposite, in fact.

She lived in splendid sumptuousness in a huge villa near the beautiful old town of Carcassonne and raised her daughter to be a lady.

It could be assumed that between Maria and her old grandfather, Don Pepe, Armanda's education had been liberally spiced with grand tales of her often absent father's patriotic deeds and the Basque "right" to a separatist homeland from Spain.

Old Don Pepe died when Armanda was twelve. Luis couldn't attend his father's funeral. He was in jail in Barcelona for leading four other Basques in a bank robbery to gain "funds of liberation."

Four years later, Luis would be dead, killed in an attempt to escape.

Between 1963 and 1969, when Armanda reached the age of eighteen, little was heard from mother or daughter.

Then, in June of 1969, Armanda married Pierre du Cort, a man forty years her senior.

The marriage lasted a year. Du Cort was killed in an auto accident on the Amalfi Drive in Italy.

He left Armanda a very wealthy widow.

For the next two years, mother and daughter petitioned Franco to allow them to return to Spain.

The answer was always no.

In retaliation Armanda toured Europe, proselytizing

against the Fascist dictator by day, and having liaisons with rich and influential men by night.

Shortly after Franco's death in 1975, the beautiful socialite married again, this time to a rich German industrialist.

Alas, this marriage also had a sad ending for the groom. He died in an airplane crash near Innsbruck.

King Juan Carlos lifted Franco's exile on the de Nerros, but Maria loudly proclaimed to all who would listen, ''. . . I will never return to the land of my fathers until it is free of Spanish tyranny!''

Evidently, Armanda agreed with her mother. The twice-widowed beauty was now fabulously wealthy. She traveled in the jettest of jet sets and used her associations to increase her wealth.

She gained a reputation as a complex woman, with deep-seated convictions about her Basque heritage as well as a seeming thirst for life in the fast lane with the very kinky and very rich of the world.

In 1979 Armanda dropped out of sight for two years. She surfaced again in 1981, in Italy. Shortly afterward, she was arrested.

Lupe de Varga was the Basque equivalent of the Palestinian terrorist and assassin, Carlos the Jackal. Acting as the Basque liaison to Italy's Red Brigade, de Varga was one of the prime movers and planners in a plot to kidnap a Swiss multimillionaire for ransom. Once the plan was carried out, the Basque separatist movement and the Red Brigade would split the proceeds to help finance further terrorist activities in their respective countries.

Before the plot could be consummated, it was uncovered. De Varga and five of his Red Brigade brothers were caught in a San Remo villa. Rather than surrender, they opted for a shoot-out with the Italian authorities.

All of them were shot and burned to cinders in one wing of

the villa. Armanda de Nerro was also in the villa. She was captured and indicted in the Italian courts for terrorist activity.

Besides being the registered owner of the villa, Armanda was rumored to have been de Varga's mistress. Because this was only rumor, and because she pleaded her innocence on the grounds that she had been kidnapped—and considering her wealth, that made sense—held against her will for months, and forced to participate, she was eventually exonerated.

Her striking beauty did not hurt her cause in an Italian courtroom, and neither did a parade of her former wealthy and influential lovers when they came forward as character witnesses.

Once her freedom was assured, de Nerro resumed her jet-setting ways on the Continent. Interpol kept track of her for a while, suspecting her continued liaison with terrorists in general and the Basque Euzkadi Ta Askatasuna in particular. When they could get nothing concrete they dropped the surveillance.

It was about then, fourteen months before, that the lady packed up, bag and baggage, and moved to Andorra with her by now aging but still active mother.

Carter closed the folder and eyeballed the steward for a fresh drink. When it came he lit a cigarette and sipped the scotch reflectively.

Armanda de Nerro was quite a woman indeed. She obviously had as much intelligence as beauty, and she had used those assets to garner a great deal of wealth and friends with influence. Combine that with a fanatical belief in a revolutionary cause like ETA, and you just might have a woman who was as deadly as she was beautiful.

But, Carter mused, was Armanda de Nerro that devoted to the Basque cause? Or were the events of her life mere accidents that made it look that way? Was her relationship with de Varga just rumor, as she claimed, or was she really his mistress and coconspirator?

Finding out would be one of Carter's main tasks.

He set aside the first folder and opened the second. It was marked *Background and current status of EUZKADI TA ASKATASUNA (ETA)—Basque revolutionary movement to create a state free of Spain*.

Carter already knew most of the folder's contents, but a few of the finer points were filled in as he read.

In the beginning, the Basques were the *gudaris,* the core strength of the Loyalist army who fought Franco. Even after the Spanish Civil War was over, the Basques took to the hills as guerrillas to fight Franco's Fascism.

Because of this they were aided and admired by a great many of the populace.

When Franco died, many thought the Basques would lay down their arms.

Nothing could have been farther from the truth. Less than twenty-four hours before democracy came to Spain under King Juan Carlos, the Basques struck against the new regime.

They executed the mayor of a small town in Guipuzcoa, an inspector of city buses, and a taxi cab driver. All were killed as "oppressors of the people."

To the Spanish people, the world at large, and their fellow Basques, this was nothing but random murder, a calling card that the new democratic government of Juan Carlos meant no more than the old Fascist regime of Franco.

In the years that followed, there were beatings, abductions, bank robberies, and extortion in the name of the Revolutionary Tax to fund the ETA terrorist movement.

By the late 1970s, ETA had declared itself a Marxist-Leninist movement. It was now dedicated to the dictatorship of the proletariat, and terrorism was the means to that end.

The leaders of ETA were no longer simply interested in Basque separatism. Their goal was continent-wide insurrection and an eventual Communist Spain.

Carter closed the folder and sighed audibly enough to turn a few heads nearby.

What better way to hold an entire country for ransom, he thought, than to threaten its government with eight missiles bearing nuclear warheads?

Carter was the last one off the plane and the first one out of the airport while the press plagued the VIPs.

He cabbed into Paris and, out of habit, changed taxis three more times before arriving at a small pension on the Left Bank.

After checking in under a cover name, he showered, shaved, and wolfed down breakfast at a nearby café.

By then it was nearly noon, the contact time Hawk had given him.

"Monsieur Pallmar, please."

The SDECE man was on the line in seconds.

"*Oui*. Pallmar."

"Monsieur Pallmar, the Vice-President's plane has landed."

"Where are you?"

"At a small café near the Pont Neuf, on the Left Bank."

"Good. Go to the St. Michel Metro station . . ."

"I know it," Carter replied.

"Get off at the Gare du Nord. There is a newsstand at the top of the Metro ramp. Ask for a copy of Baumpierre's *Revolution Today*."

"And will he have it?"

"No, but I will recognize you. Walk up the Rue de Maubeuge, cross the Boulevard de la Chapelle, and go up

Rue Stephenson toward St. Bernard. I will overtake you just short of a tiny alleyway and make contact. Follow me from there.''

"Will do.''

Carter left the café, walked the few blocks along the Seine to the Place St. Michel, and went into the Metro station. He bought a ticket and boarded the swift, silent Metro train.

At the Gare du Nord—a huge railroad station—he quickly spotted the newsstand. He perused the paperback racks for a few minutes and then made his request in French.

"Non, je regrette, monsieur. I do not have it.''

"Merci,'' Carter said and walked outside. On Rue Stephenson he slowed his pace, pausing now and then to gaze into a shop window.

He was three blocks short of the little church of St. Bernard when a small, gray-haired man in a beret and English tweeds passed near his shoulder.

"Follow me at a short distance, Monsieur Carter.''

The whisper came with barely a pause in the little man's step. Carter moved along about ten paces behind him. When the man turned into a narrow alley, Carter followed.

Fifty yards into the alley, the man stepped through a small wooden door. When Carter reached it, the door had been left partially ajar. Carter took one quick look over his shoulder and stepped through into a small courtyard.

The door closed behind him with a click, and Carter turned to see a smiling André Pallmar extending his hand.

"Sorry to make it so difficult, Monsieur Carter, but it would never do if we were seen talking in public.''

"I understand.''

"And in light of your superior's request, I hardly think it would be wise if you were seen at our offices.''

"Hardly.''

"If you will follow me, please?"

The house had three stories, the bottom two empty. The third was a series of three bedrooms, all comfortably furnished.

"Make yourself comfortable. A glass of wine?"

"Brandy, if you have it."

"Certainly."

Minutes later, the two men were settled in, drinks in hand, facing each other over a low coffee table.

"Here are the documents you will need to establish your identity as Nicholas Carstocus."

Carter examined them and smiled his appreciation at the other man. "Very thorough."

"Thank you. Needless to say, we have kept his accounts in perfect order. You may even use his credit cards. Here are several copies of his signature. I assume you have the ability, after some practice, to duplicate it perfectly?"

Carter nodded. "A small part of my training."

"Excellent. You have a photo for the passport?"

Carter produced an envelope from his inside pocket and from it a passport photo.

Pallmar took the necessary stamps, glue, and sealant from his own pockets, and two minutes later Carter's picture was on the document.

"There we are, perfect authenticity."

"I thank you, Monsieur Pallmar. And the villa?"

"Taken care of, as well as a Spanish contact in Andorra."

Again the well-manicured little hand went into the man's bottomless pockets.

"Her name is Louisa Juaneda. Vital statistics, background, and everything else you should know are on the back of the photo. Memorize it, please, and return the photo."

Carter took in the woman in one thorough glance. It was a

glamour-style composite color photo showing her in several full-length poses, with a facial close-up in the center.

Most of the full-length photos had been taken in floor-length, second-skin sequined gowns. Louisa Juaneda had lots of full-figured curves in all the right places. The close-up head shot displayed a brunette with hair so black it was almost blue, and glinting brown eyes that said, "Catch me . . . if you can!"

"Entertainer?" Carter asked.

Pallmar nodded, letting smoke stream through his nostrils from a Gauloise. "Singer. She has been working the hotel lounges in Andorra for about six months."

Carter flipped the photo and scanned the back. It was impressive. Louisa Juaneda had been working undercover for both the French and the Juan Carlos governments for almost five years, and very effectively.

Then Carter's eyes lit on her personal background, and his head jerked back up to face Pallmar.

"Basque?"

"Yes, but far from the ETA," the other man replied. "Her whole family has been financially ruined in the north of Spain because of the ETA terrorist tactics. Her father was almost killed in an ETA bombing. He lives in Madrid now, a cripple. I assure you, Monsieur Carter, she is good and can be trusted."

"Good enough for me," Carter said, passing the photo over and leaning back on the couch. "Now, how do we go about leaking me as Bluebeard?"

The cloud that passed over Pallmar's eyes hit Carter hard with its intensity. The man leaned forward and used far too much vehemence in crushing out his cigarette before he spoke at last.

"I am sure your superior has told you that we have kept Nicholas Carstocus alive—at least on paper—in the hope of netting some of his clients, or even would-be clients.''

Carter nodded and shielded the frown on his own face by lighting another cigarette of his own.

''Well, it would seem that our Mr. Carstocus entered into a contract just before we uncovered him . . .''

''And he met his untimely end.''

''Yes, a mistake that, overzealousness on the part of one of our best men. But nevertheless, Carstocus was paid a very handsome sum, probably as a down payment on a contract.''

Carter sighed. ''And now the people want some action, or their money back.''

''Quite. We have stalled them for almost a month. We were about to close the whole thing out and publicly declare Carstocus dead, when this request of yours came from Washington. Needless to say, it would be a way for you to establish yourself as Bluebeard.''

''How much was the advance?'' Carter asked.

''One hundred thousand dollars, deposited in Carstocus's Swiss account.''

''Where you can't get your hands on it.''

The narrow shoulders shrugged in the inimitable French way. ''We control his French and American accounts, but, as you say . . . the Swiss . . . ah!''

Carter stood, stretched, and began to pace.

''So if I check out the contract and agree to keep pursuing it, I might be able to hold them off long enough to get my business in Andorra done.''

''Precisely,'' Pallmar said.

''And if I don't, and if we leak Carstocus as Bluebeard, I'll have them all over my ass once I'm in Andorra.''

''Equally precise.''

''Monsieur Pallmar, I do believe I'm somewhere between the proverbial rock and a hard place.''

"A quaint American expression, Monsieur Carter, but very apt."

"Where's the contact?" Carter asked, folding his tall, catlike body back into the couch.

"Marseille," Pallmar replied, pulling a set of papers and a copy of the *International Herald Tribune* from his coat. "The name in the ad is Pepe . . ."

SIX

Carter left Paris by car on a Wednesday afternoon. Before leaving, he placed the answering ad in both the *Tribune* and *La Voix,* one of the smaller Marseille dailies.

Pepe: Prudence has caused me to take so long in replying. Say ''yes'' Friday, and check for number Saturday. Monsieur B.

He drove leisurely on the A6 to Lyon, where he spent the night, and even more slowly the next day, arriving in Avignon at around three in the afternoon.

After dumping the rented car, he cabbed to the train station, where he shipped both his bags on to Marseille in the Carstocus name.

From there he walked the few blocks to the town's old shopping quarter. From different outside stalls he made purchases of a pea jacket, two denim shirts, two pairs of faded denim trousers, a denim jacket, a pair of boots, and a heavy black turtleneck sweater.

In a surplus store he bought a duffel bag and tipped the acne-scarred young clerk to use the rest room.

Five minutes later he emerged a tramp seaman.

"We have razors, *monsieur*," the clerk said, eyeing Carter's two-day growth.

"No need," Carter growled in a low French dialect. "I'm back to sea in two days."

Carter left the shop and checked into the cheapest hotel he could find in the roughest part of town.

"Twenty francs, *monsieur*, in advance."

"Does that include a lock on the door?"

"But of course."

It did, but it didn't work. It took Carter twenty minutes to fix it, even though he knew someone could break it again in a minute if he wanted in badly enough.

Hugo—his deadly stiletto—Carter left strapped to his right calf encased in its chamois sheath. Wilhelmina and two spare clips of shells were secured under a pair of loose floorboards.

Then he stretched out on the rickety bed and, in minutes, was fast asleep.

At ten sharp his mental alarm went off. Instantly alert, he crawled from the bed and dressed in the turtleneck and denim trousers. He pulled the light denim jacket over the turtleneck and went down to the street.

The night was alive with neon and laughter from the open sidewalk cafés. On a hill dominating the city, Carter could see the Palais des Papes, the Palace of the Popes. Near it were other palaces that had been converted into modern hotels. It was there, and across the river in more expensive Villeneuve, where most of the well-heeled tourists would currently be dining and would shortly be looking for the evening's entertainment.

That, thought Carter, looking around, was exactly where he did *not* want to be.

The six-block stretch of street in front of him was perfect for the evening's hunting. It was full of garish bistros, cheap hotels—some for all-night guests, others that charged by the

hour—and three or four nightclubs with hard-looking
doormen-cum-bouncers lounging in front of their doors.

Carter moved down the street until he spotted a café that
appeared a little cleaner than the rest, and stopped. He chose
a table near the sidewalk, and waved to a dour-looking waiter
who sported a Gauloise hanging from the side of his mouth
and a dirty apron wrapped twice around his middle.

He staggered over.

"Do you wish dinner?"

"*Oui.*"

A greasy menu found its way into Carter's hands. The
waiter disappeared, and returned immediately with a glass
and a carafe of wine so thick and dark Carter wondered if it
would pour.

"What would you like, *monsieur*?"

"*Aubergine aux tomates . . . le foie de veau grillé . . .
pommes frites.*"

"I'm sorry, *monsieur*, the broiled calf's liver is not on
the menu tonight."

"I don't give a shit," Carter replied in a very low voice,
his teeth gleaming in his tanned face. "That is what I want."

"*Monsieur . . . s'il vous plaît . . .*"

The waiter reached for the menu, and Carter caught his
wrist, his nails digging into the soft inner part.

"I am celebrating my last few days ashore. I have told you
what I want to eat. Now you tell your excuse for a chef what I
want to eat."

The waiter's face was contorted with pain, and he had
clamped his jaw so hard to avoid crying out that the burning
end of the Gauloise threatened to sear his nose.

"*Oui, monsieur.*"

He skittered away, and Carter poured a glass of wine. He
lit a cigarette to go with it and leaned back to survey the
street. Streetwalkers were everywhere, a few of them obvi-

ously not straying too far from their pimps.

One caught his eye and started to move across the sidewalk. Carter shook his head, and she faded back to her corner.

There were other characters, drifters, pickpockets, a few slumming tourists, but no panhandlers.

That made him smile. Unemployed Frenchmen do not beg. They either find a job or they steal.

The food came, and he was surprised to find that it was quite good. Enough so that he left a generous tip to the waiter when he left.

He spent the next hour going from bar to bar, casing the B-girls in each of them and fending off the streetwalkers.

In an alley called Pigalle he found the place he wanted: Le Club Poupée. *Girls, Girls, Girls* and *Floor Show* danced in garish lights on the marquee, and there was a steady stream of couples going out the door and single girls going in.

"Ten francs, *monsieur* . . . cover."

Carter passed a bill through the grillwork, got a stamp on the back of his hand, and moved through the doors. The room was narrow and about fifty yards deep, with a bar the length of one side and tables along the other. A very bored-looking trio played loud music on a back bar stage, and most of the tables were occupied with women.

One tall, long-haired blonde had removed a very large breast from the front of her dress and was carefully applying rouge to the areola when Carter hit the doors.

She looked up and grinned widely as Carter passed her table. "Hallo, buy me a drink?"

"Sure."

She returned the breast to momentary safekeeping and followed Carter to a rear, unoccupied table.

He ordered whiskey. She ordered champagne that, when it came, looked like tea. He tasted it.

"Tea."

She shrugged. "I drink all night. I can't afford to get drunk. Don't worry, you'll get your money's worth."

To prove it, she reached for his crotch with a smile. Carter managed to catch her wrist and guide it back to the tabletop.

"Later."

"Good. We'll go to my place after I get off, okay?"

"Maybe."

"You a sailor?" Carter nodded, making a face as he swallowed half the whiskey. "Good, I like sailors. You'll see, I'm terrific."

Carter only smiled. It was the oldest line in the B-girl bar business. The girls never got off until three in the morning. By that time the sucker was drunk and the girl had imbibed a hundred bucks' worth of tea.

But Carter went along with it.

He partied for the next two hours, sipping whiskey and buying tea. In that time, nearly every girl in the bar had passed through the booth. He had just about given up finding the right one, when she suddenly showed up.

"I am Lily. Buy me a drink?"

In fifteen minutes the others had floated away. It was obvious that the handsome, drunken sailor had made his choice for the evening.

Carter toned down his jovial manner and loud laughter long enough to get particulars.

Her name was Lily Luciani. She was twenty-two, born in Avignon, and she was not a whore.

"I will entertain you, talk with you, drink with you . . . but I will not go to bed with you. I am a student, and this is the only job I could get."

"I think that's bloody marvelous," Carter said in low, unaccented English that made her head snap around.

"You are English?" she asked, her mouth agape.

"American, to be exact."

"But . . ."

"My French is perfect. Thank you. How much money would you ordinarily make tonight?"

"About one hundred francs . . . maybe," she stammered.

"I'll pay you that to leave with me now and have a cup of coffee."

"I told you . . ."

"A cup of coffee."

She leaned forward and, for the first time since she had sat down, stared directly into Carter's eyes. "You are sober."

"Yes, I am," he replied. "Coffee?"

"All right."

"Good, let's go. And, by the way, your English is very good."

She was petite, with a small figure that looked out of place in the tacky, cheap dress she wore. In the less garish light of the café, Carter could see that she had intelligent eyes, an upturned nose, and an almost elfin face.

Right now her neat eyebrows were arranged in a very quizzical vee.

"Let me see if I understand this. You want me to go to Marseille with you. You want it to look like a party, a seaman on his last date with his girl friend before he goes to sea."

"That's right."

"And you want me to take along two sets of clothes."

Carter nodded. "One student set, one bar girl set. Not quite as tacky as you have on. If you need anything to fill out the wardrobe, I'll buy it."

She shook her head and asked for a cigarette. Carter took one from his pack and held his lighter as she puffed awkwardly.

"You don't smoke," he said with a smile.

"I know, but I have to have something to do with my hands. I do not understand. If you need a girl for your business, why don't you hire one in Marseille?"

"Simple. What I want done won't be dangerous for you while I'm around. It could be when I'm gone. A girl in Marseille might be found after I'm gone. You won't be found in Avignon."

"Why me? Why not one of the other girls?"

Carter's grin broadened. "Do you think you're smarter than those other girls?"

She hesitated but finally replied. "Yes."

"There's your answer. I need someone who needs the money and is willing to go to certain lengths to get it."

"And any girl who would work in Le Club Poupée would go to certain lengths?"

"I think so," Carter said.

Another long pause, and then Lily leaned forward and spoke in a low, throaty voice. "Are you a policeman?"

"No."

"A crook?"

"No."

"But this business you are talking about . . . it is . . . illegal."

"That's what you're going to help me find out."

She leaned back and sighed in exasperation. "You are not a sailor."

"No."

"Then why . . . ?"

"If I had walked into your club in a business suit, thrown my money around, and walked out with you, how many of those girls would have remembered me?"

"All of them!" she said firmly and then swallowed. "Ten thousand francs?"

"Half now, if you want it."

"No, I . . . I don't know why, but I trust you."

He grinned. "It's probably because I'm an American. Get your things. I'll meet you at the train station in two hours."

"All right, I'll go. But, remember, I won't screw you!"

The Hotel Vincennes on the Quai Port was cheap, and the management paid very little attention to its patrons as long as the rent was paid in advance.

Carter stayed well behind her from the train station to the port, then killed an hour over breakfast and harsh coffee after she checked in. When he was sure there would be little connection between them, he made his way into the old-fashioned but fairly clean lobby of the hotel.

A bored concierge-desk clerk-bellboy answered the bell and barely glanced at Carter as he whirled the register around.

"Without bath?"

"With," Carter replied, signing "Napoleon Bonaparte III" to the register with a flourish.

The man spun the big book back around, glanced down, and then looked up at Carter with a scowl.

"Monsieur is in the entertainment business? . . . A comedian, perhaps?"

"Monsieur is trying to get a ship after he became slightly drunk and missed the sailing of his last one."

"I see. Then you have no passport?"

It was a fairly common thing among seamen, but nevertheless dangerous. If a merchant seaman missed his ship and was without papers, he had to apply to the *Français Maritime National* for new ones and be incarcerated until he was on another ship.

"Passport?" Carter smiled. "Of course . . . right here!"

He laid two one-hundred-franc notes on the desk between

them. The man's hand came out like a mongoose striking and the notes disappeared.

"The room is two hundred and forty francs a night, *monsieur . . .* in advance, of course."

"Of course."

Carter laid out three more big ones. They went into a drawer and no change was offered.

"*Merci, monsieur.* Room five-oh-one."

Carter took the key and made a detour through the hotel café on his way to the elevator.

Lily, following his instructions to the letter, was seated alone near the entrance. He dropped his duffel bag at the door and crossed the room.

"*Calvados, ma petite, s'il vous plaît.*"

The woman behind the counter selected the bottle, wrapped it, and took his money. Carrying the bottle of apple brandy, Carter moved back through the tables. Passing Lily, he let his eyes flicker downward for the briefest of seconds.

Good girl, he thought.

Right beside her plate was a napkin. On it was written 412. One step beyond the table he saw her take the napkin, dab her lips, and carelessly slide it into her purse.

Going up in the elevator, Carter sighed with relief. He had made a good choice.

In the room, he unpacked, poured three fingers of the brandy into a glass, and sat down to write out the ad.

Pepe: Phone 391-444 at 5 sharp Saturday P.M. Monsieur B.

He waited another twenty minutes to make sure Lily had time to return to her room, and then he took the stairs down to the fourth floor.

His knuckles had barely brushed the veneered wood before

the door opened and Carter popped inside.

"This is fun!" Lily said, her dark eyes flashing with excitement and an elfin grin on her face.

"Don't let it be too much fun," Carter said grimly. "Here."

He passed her the scrap of paper then spread a map of Marseille out on the bed.

"I'll leave first. You follow in exactly thirty minutes. The newspaper office is here, Number Eight rue Montparnasse. Take a taxi. After you place the ad, leave the office and walk down to the corner . . . here. That will put you on the Avenue du Prado. At Bond Point, turn right. At Arménienne, here, go in and pray."

"Pray?"

"That's what I said . . . for about twenty minutes. When you leave there, take a cab to the Baraly Museum, here."

"And that's where I play the whore?"

"Exactly. There is a little café just across the street, here. Take him there. And, remember, you'll be followed, but at no time look over your shoulder as if you were looking for it. Do you understand everything?"

She nodded.

"Good. Just be natural. I'll be close by all the time."

From a hallway in an office building across the street, Carter watched Lily enter the newspaper offices. The business took only about ten minutes, and soon she was out again, strolling toward the Avenue du Prado.

She looked good in a striped black and white pullover that stretched tautly across her breasts, and a black, shimmering skirt that hugged her hips and bottom like a second skin.

With spike heels, a beret, and mesh stockings, she looked just tacky enough to pull it off.

He could have brought in an experienced operative from

the Paris AXE headquarters, but that would have taken time. And there was a good chance that little Lily could perform better anyway. True, there was the risk factor, but with only two small things to perform—and Carter himself on her like glue—it was unlikely anything dangerous would happen.

He watched her turn at the Avenue du Prado, then shifted his concentration back to the newspaper offices.

An untrained eye might not have seen such an infinitesimal change.

Carter didn't miss it.

Above the doorway was a large clock. Just beneath the clock's face was a three-by-four-foot digital readout of the current temperature.

It had been blinking regularly since his arrival. It was now turned off.

It didn't take much looking. They were at a sidewalk table in the café directly below Carter. One was a short, paunchy man with a thick shock of black hair that seemed to be constantly tumbling over his eyes. The other was a little taller but lean as a reed and nattily dressed in a beige gabardine suit. His arresting feature was a horribly pockmarked face and dark eyes that seemed to recede clear inside his skull.

The short, fat one, a paper under his arm, took the point after Lily. The second waited several minutes to see if his comrade was followed.

When he was sure this was not the case, he picked up the trail himself.

Carter made the rear of the building in less than two minutes. He had already reconned the cab stand in the middle of the block. It had not been left unoccupied in the twenty minutes he had been checking it.

And it wasn't now.

"Eglise Arménienne?"

"Oui."

"An extra thirty francs," Carter added in French, "if you make it in five minutes or less."

The G-force of the leaping taxi put him hard against the seat and kept him there for the full three-minute ride.

There was a newsstand directly across from the church. Carter made for it and browsed through racks of paperbacks until he spotted Lily.

Without any hesitation, she walked up the steps and entered the cathedral.

They were exactly thirty seconds behind her, with the taller one now in front. Both of them went a block beyond the church, where they paused at a storefront and conferred out of the sides of their mouths.

Short and pudgy was elected. He returned and entered the cathedral.

Carter did not wait. He purchased the Paris edition of an American skin magazine and took to the street.

Two blocks past the hollow-eyed window watcher, Carter turned onto Rue Paradis and found another cab.

"Musée Baraly?"

"*Oui.*"

"Take your time," Carter said, easing back into the seat and lighting a cigarette.

Carter sat, sipping brandy and espresso, in the café directly across the street from the Baraly Museum. Lily had entered the building nearly a half hour earlier. Her two watchdogs were close behind.

Now he watched her crossing the street arm in arm with a tall, athletic specimen in a dark blue, conservatively cut suit. He was about six-three, with wide-set blue eyes, a tanned and seamed face, and just the right amount of steel gray at the temples to give him age and a little class.

He did not have the look of the typical killer. But then Bluebeard wouldn't have.

An excellent choice, Carter thought, one eye on the magazine, the other on the couple.

They sat down three tables away, just close enough for Carter to hear part of their conversation.

Acne-face entered and took a table by the window. Short and pudgy made for a phone booth near the museum steps.

Bingo, Carter thought, and sipped his brandy.

"I am just a working girl, *monsieur*," Lily was saying, "not a whore."

"Oh, my dear, I'm sure of that. But I am sure you wouldn't turn down a slight gift for your favors . . . ?"

"Of course not," Lily said and smiled coquettishly.

"Then, shall we go? My apartment is just around the corner."

Lily shot a quick look out of the corner of her eye at Carter.

He returned the look with a barely perceptible shake of his head while sipping from the cup of espresso. Whoever short and pudgy was talking to on the phone, Carter wanted them to have plenty of time to arrive.

Lily played it to the hilt. A seasoned actress—or courtesan—couldn't have done it much better.

When the mark began to get too insistent about leaving, she played him along by running her hand up his thigh under the table. When he got too amorous, she got slightly angry, and when he showed signs of cooling off, she whispered all the erotic things she was capable of performing.

When Carter saw the black limousine pick up short and pudgy and move on down the block, he moved to the counter and paid his check.

Lily was already up and moving toward the ladies' room in

the rear. She would go on through the hall and exit a rear door into the alley.

Her would-be lover was rubbing his hands together at the table.

Carter donned sunglasses and tugged his knit watch cap down over his forehead when he hit the street. Passing the limo he made the license number, but the windows were blacked out with dark glass, making it impossible to read the occupants.

He walked a measured, slow pace to the corner, but once around, he broke into a sprint. Around the second corner he spotted Lily waiting nervously at the mouth of the alley.

"Was he all right?"

"Perfect. Did you get the address?"

"Eight Rue Celese . . . a block down and four doors to the right."

"You're an angel," Carter said, pecking her on the lips. "Get back to the hotel. I'll see you later."

Carter took off at a dead run. He made three blocks, turned, and then doubled back until he spotted Rue Celese. Two doors down from Number 8 and across the street was a "To Let" sign.

He rang the bell.

"Oui?" She was a harridan, about sixty, with huge, pendulous breasts, huger hips, and blue hair coiled on top of her head.

"I would like to see the rooms."

The woman looked at his clothes, his unshaven face, and started to close the door.

Carter managed to wedge his body between the door and the jamb. At the same time, he produced a thick wad of bills with the hundred-franc notes in clear sight.

"Actually, madame, I would like to use the apartment for about a half hour."

"Monsieur, you are insane."

Carter peeled off two bills, one hundred francs each, and pressed them into her pudgy hand.

"An affair of the heart, madame. I have been at sea for nearly a year. I return . . . my wife . . . a scoundrel . . ."

He accented his words with the French shrug. She hesitated but also shrugged when Carter added a third bill.

"Two-A, directly above. The door is open. And don't smoke, *monsieur.* I have just cleaned."

"Madame, I only want a place to set my eyes."

It was twenty minutes before tall and athletic came around the corner with a smile on his face and a spring in his step. The limo was nowhere in sight, but Carter knew it soon would be.

The would-be lover entered Number 8, and one minute later the limo sailed by and parked at the corner. Lily's two watchdogs jumped out and returned to Number 8.

They were efficient. The poor guy barely got out two words before they were through the door.

Five minutes later, the short one was out the door and heading for the limo for instructions. They were short, and in no time he was back in the flat.

Carter smiled to himself. If Pepe was as sharp as he should be, it would not take him longer than five minutes on his car phone to see that the lothario in Number 8 was a far cry from Bluebeard.

It took three minutes.

They both came out the door and made for the limo on the dead run.

Carter waited fifteen more minutes, then headed down the stairs.

The old lady was standing in the open door of her apartment. "Well?"

"Well," Carter said and shrugged. "I guess she decided

not to visit him today.''

He cabbed to the Vieux Port and found a phone booth before returning to the hotel.

The call to Paris went through at once.

''Pallmar here.''

''This is the man from Washington.''

''Yes.''

''I have a license number of a motor vehicle in Marseille.''

''What is it?''

''F-S-S-X-four-four-one.''

''And the number of your phone?'' Carter read off the number of the pay phone. ''Five minutes.''

The connection died, and he lit a cigarette to wait.

It was a long shot but one worth trying. Carter guessed that whoever Pepe was, he was the go-between for the party buying the hit. If Nels Pomroy was Bluebeard's broker, the chances were pretty good that Pepe did not know Bluebeard's real identity.

That was why tall and handsome had taken some abuse that afternoon. If Carter could get a name, the cards were in his corner.

The jangling phone brought him back.

''Yes.''

''The car is registered to Marc LeClerc. He has a residence in Nice and one in Marseille on the Rue Emile Zola . . . Number thirty-seven.''

''And what does Monsieur LeClerc do to occupy his time?''

''On the surface he is a munitions broker.''

''And underneath?''

''He is the banker for the Basque revolutionary front, Euzkadi Ta Askatasuna.''

Lily was pacing the room like a caged animal when Carter

made his way down from his own room and deposited food and a bottle of wine on the bed.

"I saw those men."

"Did you?" Carter said, biting into a loaf of bread and stuffing bits of cheese and roast beef into his mouth.

"They looked like killers."

"Did they?"

"Damn you, what is this all about?"

Carter set the food down and pulled the wad of bills from his pocket. He peeled off ten one-thousand-franc notes and placed them on the bed.

"A bargain is a bargain."

"Who are you?" she said, standing before him, chewing on her lower lip.

"I'm a man with a job . . . a strange job, but just a job."

He added two more bills to the stack and chewed off another hunk of bread.

"We'll stay put until tomorrow evening's phone calls. Once that's done, it's back to Avignon with you and a comfortable life for a while."

"And that is all I am to know?"

"That's all. Eat, the cheese is good."

She nibbled and sipped the wine until Carter had eaten his fill.

She watched him with wide, almost fearful eyes as he stood and stretched.

"Where are you going?"

"Back to my room. It's late and there'll be a lot to do before the phone call tomorrow afternoon." He leaned over and lightly brushed his lips over her forehead. "Good night, my little student."

In his own room, Carter stripped, then slipped Hugo under his pillow and Wilhelmina under the bed.

Between the sheets, he was asleep in five minutes, only to

be awakened by a light tap on the door.

He slid from the bed and flattened himself against the wall by the door with Wilhelmina in his hand.

"Yes?"

"It's me . . . Lily."

Carter growled, then slipped the chain and turned the bolt.

The door was barely ajar before she slipped through it and closed it behind her.

"Where are you . . . ?"

"Right behind you," Carter said, lightly touching her shoulder.

"Oh! . . . oh."

"What is it?"

"I'm afraid."

"Oh, Christ, this is a fine time to be afraid."

"I do not mean I am afraid of tomorrow . . ."

"What then?"

"I am afraid of tonight."

Carter frowned. "Well, what do you want me to do about it?"

"Let me stay here with you."

"I thought you said . . ."

"That I would not make love to you? I will not. But I did not say I would not sleep with you."

Wearily, Carter stumbled to the bed and crawled between the sheets. "Suit yourself."

He heard her undressing in the darkness. Then he felt her weight shift the bed and the tug of the covers.

He was almost asleep when she slithered across the bed and molded her body to his.

"I am not afraid now."

"Good."

Silence.

"Do you want to make love to me?"

"If I say yes, you'll say no," Carter replied. "If I say no, your feelings will be hurt. Right?"

"I . . . I guess so."

"So I won't say anything."

She wriggled her soft, round bottom into his belly and found his hand. He did not try to stop her when he felt the full, firm mound of one of her breasts fill his palm.

"What *is* your name?"

He thought for a moment and decided it didn't make a hell of a lot of difference. "Nick."

"Nick?"

"Yes."

"I am not afraid now."

"Good. Good night."

"Good night."

She was sound asleep at least two hours before he was.

SEVEN

The bribe is useful all over the world. When one knows how to use it and can find someone susceptible to it, the options are unlimited.

That was why Lily was needed for Carter's operation to penetrate Pepe. Anyone who was brokering killers in the Bluebeard class could be expected to have someone inside the newspaper offices who would tip him off when a certain ad was placed.

It would be just as easy for him to obtain the location of a phone number, whether it be private or a phone booth.

For that reason, Carter stood just inside the high wall on the third tier of the Ganay Stadium. To the east, south, and north were the open areas of the parking lots for the stadium, Chanot Park, and the Palais des Expositions. To the east were the wide boulevards of the Marguerite district, with their sidewalk cafés, restaurants, bistros, and chic women's wear shops.

From his perch on the soccer stadium wall, Carter could see nearly a mile in every direction. Right now, through a pair of high-powered binoculars, he could see Lily calmly sipping coffee in a café at the corner of Place Michelet and Boulevard Leon. She wore a bright red skirt and a thin white summer sweater that could be spotted easily from any distance.

At the edge of the sidewalk, four paces from her table, was a phone booth. The number of the booth was the number Carter had placed in the ad.

It was five minutes to five, and Pepe's boys were already in place. They sat just across the square from Lily in a dark gray Cortina.

Carter could see them talking to one another without ever shifting their eyes from Lily. They spoke like a pair of old cons, their lips barely moving.

Carter guessed that was exactly what they were.

The black limousine was nowhere in sight, but Carter didn't figure it would be. Pepe or Marc LeClerc would not risk being spotted by Bluebeard twice without knowing what the killer's intentions were.

Carter saw a flash of red in the corner of the glasses, and he shifted back to Lily. She was on her feet and moving toward the booth.

Farther down the block, short and pudgy started the Cortina.

Carter waited until Lily was finished on the phone and was back at her table before sprinting down the three levels of stone stairs to the stadium entrance.

He was pretty sure the men in the Cortina would eventually make a try for Lily, but not while she was in the crowded café.

His heels had barely touched the cement of the first level when the phone near the entrance started ringing.

Carter was in the booth in three strides. He yanked the instrument from its cradle and took a deep breath. Now came the moment of truth. Had Carstocus—as Bluebeard—ever made contact directly with Pepe, or had it always been through Pomroy?

And if that contact had been made, would Pepe recognize Carstocus's voice?

"Bluebeard here."

"This is Pepe. What are you trying to pull?"

Carter relaxed. "I'm being safe. I don't know you, and Pomroy has disappeared."

"We think he is dead. Why haven't you delivered on the contract?"

Again Carter tensed. Now came the second shot in the dark.

"I never received the vitals."

"You *what*?"

"Just what I said," Carter replied, confidence flowing now like a fast river through his body. "I never got the particulars or the target from Nels."

"Damnit, you received the money!"

"True, and I'm willing to fulfill the contract. Give me a number where I can reach you. We'll set up a meet."

"You must be insane! Part of our arrangement was that we never meet . . . no faces, no names."

"That was your arrangement with Pomroy. Now it's a new deal."

"Impossible!"

"Then no deal."

There was a long pause on the other end of the line. Carter guessed that a hand was being held over the receiver because he could distinguish muffled voices in the background.

Then Pepe was back.

"I take it you still want the contract?"

"Yes, on my terms."

"We are not a wealthy organization. We have given you a great deal of money. If we can't come to an agreement, what happens to the half you have already received?"

"It stays in my Swiss accounts."

Another pause with more background voices.

"Very well. Do you have a pencil?"

"I have a good memory."

Pepe rattled off a number. "What time will you call?"

"I don't know. Just stay by the phone."

Pepe was cursing in a mixture of French and Spanish as Carter broke the connection. He quickly dropped the required coins into the slot and waited for Lily to answer.

"Yes?"

"It's me. Everything's right on schedule. Wait ten minutes and then take off. And do exactly as I told you. Okay?"

"Okay," she replied with only a hint of fear in her voice.

"Don't worry, luv, it's almost all over."

He replaced the instrument and jogged back up the stairs.

There was anger and frustration all over the two faces in the Cortina. Lily was visibly nervous, but she was holding fast at the table, her eyes darting to the watch on her wrist every few seconds.

"Just do it like I wrote it, honey," Carter whispered, his eyes watering a bit behind the glasses.

Then she was up and moving across the square, the Cortina crawling along about two blocks back.

For the next hour Lily wandered along the fringes of the park. She bought a newspaper, sat on a bench and played at reading it, and even fed some ducks in a small pond.

Then, at precisely 5:50, with the sun starting to dip, she crossed Boulevard Michelet and entered the narrow streets and alleyways that would eventually lead her to the promenade along the docks.

Short and pudgy left the Cortina to keep track of her on foot, and his buddy slid over into the driver's seat.

They were good, Carter mused, following them with the glasses until they were out of sight: good but predictable.

Carter moved down to the street and hailed a cab.

"Nouvelle Plage."

"*Oui, monsieur.*"

It would take Lily, walking, about thirty minutes to cover the distance the cab did in five.

"Stop here," Carter said when they reached the point on the promenade he had already staked earlier that day. "Do you see that alley there that runs alongside the racetrack?"

"*Oui, monsieur.*"

"In twenty minutes, a woman will come out of there wearing a white sweater and a red skirt. Pick her up and take her where she wants to go."

"Twenty minutes it is."

Carter fluttered the torn half of a five-hundred-franc note in the driver's face. "She will have the other half of this."

Carter looked over his shoulder and saw a beaming smile on the cab driver's face.

As he jogged across the promenade, he entered the maze of alleys that adjoined the racetrack, passed the paddocks, and broke into a run across the wide walkway to Baraly Park.

He could see Lily just entering the park on the opposite side. Short and pudgy was about a block behind her, and the Cortina was about twenty yards behind him. Both of them were closing fast.

Carter had guessed right.

They knew the city and had picked the best spot to take her: a narrow lane between two hedgerows about halfway through the park.

Carter made the lane first and moved into one of the many alcoves in the hedge that housed benches and statuary. A few hours from now, under cover of complete darkness, the alcove would become a meeting place for a pair of young lovers.

Right now Carter had a very different use for it.

He could hear Lily's heels clicking on the narrow walk,

getting louder and louder, until she flashed past. She did not glance into the alcove, but then she would not know which one he had chosen, and in the pea jacket and dark sweater he was almost invisible.

Close on her heels, his pace increasing with every step, came her pursuer.

Carter rolled his weight to the balls of his feet and tensed to spring.

He saw a coat sleeve and then a short, stocky body.

"Monsieur . . . ."

"Oui? . . . Que . . . ?"

Carter's clenched hands, forming one powerful fist, came down smack in the center of the man's face. He felt and heard the nose go, and just as a cry of pain rolled from the man's smashed lips, Carter grasped him by the lapels.

In one swift, deft movement he whirled, ramming the small of the man's back against the edge of the fountain. A second howl of pain was cut off as the side of Carter's hand came down across the back of his neck.

Like wet laundry, the body folded to the brick floor of the alcove, but Carter was already in the lane walking toward the headlights of the Cortina. A cigarette was in his mouth, and his hands cupped the flame of a match.

About ten yards from the crawling car, Carter squinted through the smoke streaming from his nostrils. The driver's dark, deep-set eyes were darting everywhere looking for his mate.

By the time Carter was directly alongside the car's open window, he had sucked the cigarette between his lips into a glowing ember.

"Hey, you . . . !"

The pockmarked face turned directly toward him just as Carter flipped the cigarette. The ash hit the bridge of the guy's nose and spread. Some of it must have caught one or both eyes, because the howl from his throat was blood-curdling.

But he was game.

He must have been rolling along in neutral, because when his foot hit the accelerator nothing happened but a lot of rpm's and no movement.

Before he could find the gear shift, Carter had the door open and had grabbed a handful of his hair. As Carter yanked, the guy tried to claw a PPK from beneath his jacket.

It was a mistake for two reasons.

One, the pistol had a long, cumbersome silencer screwed into its snout. The end of the silencer caught on his jacket and wouldn't let go.

Two, he had thumbed the safety off when he tried to pull it.

Carter heard the *phfft* sound, and the guy was dead weight in his hands. He flipped him over, and when he saw the dark stain clear across his chest, Carter did not even bother to check for a pulse.

He hit the dash button to release the trunk lid and dragged the body to the rear of the car. When he had it stuffed as far inside as it would go, he lifted the guy's wallet.

As he jogged back to the alcove, he emptied the wallet into the pea jacket—ID and miscellaneous cards in the left pocket, cash in the right.

When short and pudgy was stuffed in with his buddy, Carter did the same with his wallet, then threw the two pieces of leather in with the bodies and slammed the trunk lid.

Lily was waiting under a streetlight at the foot of the Musée Baraly steps.

"Get in!"

She did, and sat, white-faced and rigid, as Carter pulled into traffic on the boulevard and headed for the train station.

"Where are they?" she asked at last in a surprisingly calm voice.

"In the trunk."

"Are they . . . are they . . . dead?"

Carter barely made a yellow and pushed the little car up to fifty on the Corniche J.F. Kennedy before flicking her a quick, sidelong glance.

Her jaw was set in a hard line, and her complexion was an ashy white. But she was not trembling, and there was no sign of hysteria.

"Are they?" she asked again, turning her face toward him but unable to meet his eyes.

"No," Carter half lied, then he checked his watch. It was 7:00 sharp. The train to Avignon would leave at 7:14.

"They are evil men, aren't they?"

"Yes," Carter said, "they are."

"Then it is all right . . . what you have done."

"Am doing," he corrected and threw her another quick glance. Her fragile lips were trying to smile.

Ahh, youth, he thought, whipping the car into the station drive.

He rolled on past the entrance into shadows, stopped, and tugged her purse from her hands. Pulling the wads of money from the right-hand pocket of his pea jacket, he stuffed the whole amount into the purse.

"What is that?"

"A little bonus," Carter replied, dropping the purse in her lap. "It will replace your bag and clothes at the hotel. *Adieu.*"

"Just *adieu* . . . ?"

"That's it," he replied, looking straight ahead. "That's got to be it."

She leaned across the seat and turned his face to hers with one hand. With the other she stuffed a piece of paper into his hand as she kissed him.

It was a short but sensitive kiss that said a lot without promising anything.

And then she was standing outside the car, her face obscured in the shadow from the building.

"What's this?"

"My address . . . my telephone number in Avignon. Perhaps one day . . ."

She left it hanging and turned away.

Carter watched her all the way through the station before he lit a cigarette and pulled the Cortina back into traffic.

Rue Emile Zola was a narrow, tree-lined street in one of Marseille's more posh and older residential districts. The estates were large and set far back from the road in the midst of heavy shrubs and towering, leafy trees.

Number 37 was not a great deal different than its neighbors, except that its huge wrought-iron gates fronted just across from a side street that angled up a hill.

Carter smiled when he noticed this and lightly ran his fingertips over the small electronic device clipped to the sun visor above his head.

He made two passes in front of the gates, then turned into the side street and climbed until he could look down into the property behind him. When he was satisfied, he made a U-turn, parked, and killed the headlights.

With the binoculars he studied the layout.

A thick, crenelated wall ran around the entire perimeter of the property. The house itself was massive. Architecturally, it was a bastard cross between an English Tudor mansion and a French country château.

To the right, where the stables had once been, three sets of open double doors now revealed a garage. On the left was a swimming pool, and beyond that were a pair of tennis courts.

Monsieur LeClerc's organization might be pleading poverty, Carter thought, but the gentleman himself certainly managed to live in style.

A wide, asphalt lane led straight down from the gate to a

courtyard and the main entrance of the house. The Mercedes limousine and a dark blue Citroën station wagon with Paris VLT plates sat near the marble steps leading up to the front portal.

Satisfied that his little plan of surprise had at least a ninety-five percent chance of success, Carter moved to the rear of the Cortina.

"Hey, sleeping beauty," he whispered, tapping lightly on the lid with the silencer of the Walther.

There was no response.

He opened the trunk with the keys and felt short and pudgy's pulse. It was faint but still there.

"Well, little man," Carter said, "if you survive the crash, you're going to have a lot of explaining to do to your boss."

He dragged both bodies—one dead, one breathing—from the trunk and propped them up in the back seat. When they were secured with the seat belts, he closed the trunk lid and crawled back behind the wheel.

Everything had to be arranged just so.

The electronic gate opener he held in his left hand. The PPK—with the safety safely on—he tucked into his belt.

Then he started the Cortina.

"Ready, gentlemen?" he growled, glancing at his passengers in the rearview mirror.

Hollow-eyes stayed that way. Short and pudgy's lips were twisted into a grotesque grin.

"Good show . . . we're off!"

He rolled forward in low, then pressed the accelerator halfway as he shifted into second.

Fifty yards short of the bottom of the hill, he pointed the little gray instrument forward, pushed the "open" button, and sighed with relief as the huge iron gates rolled inward.

At the edge of Rue Emile Zola, he floored the car for two seconds, then shifted into neutral.

Ten feet short of the gate he rolled from the car and hit the soft, grassy ditch in a tuck.

One roll brought him to his knees and then to his toes. Without a second's pause, he scrambled back up the drive.

The Cortina was already through the opening and careening directly down the hill toward the courtyard.

Carter hit the "close" button, and the gates swung swiftly and silently shut. The latch had barely clicked before he was pumping shells into the black box just inside the gate that controlled the electric eye.

When the Walther clicked on empty, he threw it and the gate opener over the wall and took off in a sprint up the hill.

He did not turn around until he heard the crash. By that time he was in the darkness at the top of the hill.

The smile that creased his face was pure satisfaction as he crouched on one knee and brought the glasses to his eyes.

The Cortina had sideswiped the Citroën and kissed grille to grille with the Mercedes. The bigger, heavier, and better-made car was far from out of commission, but cosmetically it was a mess.

There had been only two or three lights on in the house. Now it was like a Christmas tree, and men were pouring through the front door and around the side of the house from the garage.

Two of them assessed the situation in the Cortina instantly. They both looked toward the now closed gate, gestured, and sprinted toward the Citroën. The driver's side door was unopenable, so they both had to get into the car through the passenger side.

In no time they had the car started and were roaring up the hill toward the gate.

Through the glasses, in the Citroën's dashboard lights, Carter could see the man on the right feverishly pumping the button on an electronic device similar to the one Carter had just used and tossed over the wall.

When both men realized that the gate was not going to work, the driver slammed on his brakes. The sound of screaming tires broke the night stillness, and the car rocked to a halt with its front bumper inches from the gate.

Carter replaced the glasses in their case under his arm and jogged on over the hill. Sure now that there would be no pursuit, he slowed to a leisurely walk when he hit a main boulevard and made for the port.

About a mile from Rue Emile Zola, he stepped into a small bistro. Inside, there was a young crowd, mostly college age. They sat at tables surrounding a small stage where a girl strummed a guitar and sang a lamentation about the state of French politics.

"*Monsieur?*"

"*Calvados, s'il vous plaît.*"

"*Oui, monsieur.*"

Carter sipped the brandy and smoked for the next twenty minutes.

"Is there a phone?"

"In the rear, *monsieur*, in the Gentlemen's."

"*Merci.*"

Carter made his way down a dark hallway and entered the men's room. Inside, he checked the two booths, found them empty, and dropped coins into the phone.

"*Oui?*" It was answered on the second ring.

Carter squeezed his nostrils with a thumb and forefinger and spoke with his tongue hitting his teeth to simulate a lisp.

"*Monsieur LeClerc, s'il vous plaît.*"

"*Un moment.*"

LeClerc's voice, raspy with tension, was on the line in ten seconds.

"Yes?"

"Monsieur LeClerc?"

"Yes, yes, who is this?"

Carter dropped the lisp and removed the fingers from his nose.

"This, Pepe, is Bluebeard."

The silence from the other end of the line was like a tomb. Carter waited until he was sure that LeClerc had digested the fact that his cover for Pepe was blown, then he spoke again.

"Did you get my message, LeClerc?"

"So it was you. I suspected as much. Did you have to kill Petri to make your point?"

"I didn't. It was an accident. He killed himself. How about the other one?"

"A broken back."

"Too bad," Carter said. "The misfortunes of a dangerous business. You should have called them off."

"I think it's clear why I didn't. You now have the advantage of knowing who I am, and I know nothing about you."

"In fairness, LeClerc, I am willing to rectify that. If you see my face and can identify me, will that give you some insurance that I plan on carrying out my part of the bargain?"

"I think that would be acceptable."

"Good. Do you know the vista drive above the Hippodrome?"

"Of course, the Pont de Vivaux."

"Very well. Tomorrow morning, I want you to drive to the very top . . . just you and a driver."

"What time?"

"The forecasters tell us that sunrise tomorrow will be at six fifty-eight. Shall we say, two minutes past dawn?"

"Agreed."

"Au revoir, monsieur," Carter said. "Sleep well!"

He moved back through the bistro, pausing only long enough to drop a few bills on the bar.

Three blocks away, he hailed a cab and rode directly to the

Vieux Port and the hotel.

"Wait," Carter said to the cab driver, dropping some francs over the seat.

"Oui, monsieur."

He took the tiny elevator to the fifth floor and walked down to the fourth. It took less than five minutes to gather all of Lily's things and take them back to his room, where he packed them in his own duffel bag.

At the desk, Carter dropped the keys in the slot and regained the taxi.

"La gare principle, s'il vous plaît."

It was ten minutes to the main railway station. There he paid the cabbie and made directly for the transient bag claim area.

"Your claim check, *monsieur?"*

The old man paid little attention to the seedy-looking sailor picking up the two very expensive leather bags. Carter tipped him just enough francs to keep him happy but not enough to crease his memory.

A block from the station he deposited the duffel bag in a large garbage container and continued on to the public baths.

A half hour later he emerged, clean-shaven, in a conservative black suit with gray pinstripes, soft leather loafers from Italy that could not be purchased anywhere for less than two hundred dollars, and a crisp white-on-white shirt with a narrow, unpatterned indigo tie.

On the street, he shunned a cab and walked the ten blocks to an all-night rent-a-car.

"I ordered a car by phone this morning," he said, passing over his passport and credit card.

"Oui, monsieur. It is ready for you."

An attendant loaded the car with his bags while Carter filled out the papers under the clerk's watchful and appreciative eyes.

It was not often he had a customer who could afford a month's rental on a forty-thousand-dollar automobile.

The doorman was just as appreciative of Carter's style of arrival when he pulled into the drive from Rue la Canebière and rocked the impressive little car to a halt in front of the Hotel Grand et Noailles.

The crisply attired concierge waited behind the huge mahogany desk with a beaming smile.

"May I be of assistance, *monsieur*?"

"You may. I have a suite reserved."

"The name, *monsieur*?"

"Carstocus. Nicholas Carstocus."

EIGHT

Nick Carter stood on the very edge of the cliff, smoke rolling slowly from the corners of his lips. Against the misty dawn sky he made a clear and easy target.

He meant to.

LeClerc would feel much easier because of it.

Far below him, the city of Marseille had already come to boiling life. Autos jammed the corniche leading to the docks, and commuter traffic flowed inward on the city's two northern arteries from the port city's suburbs.

He heard the low rumble of a powerful engine behind him and flipped the cigarette in a high arc over the edge of the cliff. Other than the movement of his arm, he was still. Even his eyes did not blink when the front bumper of the Mercedes rocked to a halt a scant six inches from the back of his legs.

He heard the door open and then the soft pad of feet over the grassy earth.

"Are you armed?" a voice, just behind and to his left, asked in slightly accented English.

"Yes, a Luger. Shoulder holster, left side."

A hand snaked under his jacket, and Carter felt the weight of Wilhelmina lifted from her soft leather sheath.

Only when the hands had completed a quick frisk of his waist and down his legs did Carter finally turn.

The Mercedes's front bumper was an inverted vee, the grille was a mangled mess, and the fronts of both fenders were pleated beyond repair.

"A pity," Carter smiled. "Such a marvelous machine."

"*Basta!*" the dark little man hissed and motioned Carter to the rear, passenger side of the limousine.

Carter slid into the rear seat, and the door slammed behind him. He heard the unmistakable click of the electronic door locks and calmly lit a cigarette.

"Monsieur Bluebeard, at last," the man said in French.

"Monsieur LeClerc . . . and, I assume, Pepe?"

"I think it is far from an assumption on your part, *monsieur*. My congratulations on your cunning."

He was about sixty, with an earnest, fleshy face. His wiry, sleek black hair was just receding on each side of the crown and had only a touch of gray in the sideburns. His skin seemed to sag like the rest of him, but his eyes were black pinpoints of alert intelligence.

A whirring sound closed the window between the front and rear seats. That, coupled with the blacked-out windows, threw the rear of the car into near darkness.

LeClerc's hand moved to a console between them, and a dome light and lights in the doors came on.

For the first time, Carter noticed a thin manila envelope in the man's lap.

"I must say, I admire your courage if not your methods. My driver could have shot you where you stood when we drove up."

"He could have," Carter agreed.

"And letting yourself be relieved of your gun takes a lot of nerve."

"Not really."

LeClerc took time to study Carter before speaking again. He perceived the wide shoulders, the powerful chest, and then he met the other's eyes with his own. Carter's eyes seemed to look completely through him, sifting as they penetrated.

A barely perceptible chill seemed to slice through LeClerc's body. In his lifetime he had dealt with many men whose eyes held the icy chill he saw now.

Always there was a killer behind them.

"How so?" LeClerc said at last.

"I really don't need a gun to kill you or your little appendage in the front seat, LeClerc. I could do it with my bare hands. And if they failed, there is always this . . ."

Carter tensed the muscles in his right forearm to activate the spring in Hugo's sheath. The thin stiletto shot from his cuff, the hilt settling comfortably in his right palm.

The driver had been watching his every movement in the rearview mirror. When he saw the blade in Carter's hand, he activated the window and pawed for his gun.

The window had slid less than an inch when Carter jammed Hugo's point into its catch, arresting its downward movement.

LeClerc's hand came up to calm his driver, and a thin smile creased his wide face.

"Once again, you prove your point quite well."

Carter shrugged. "It is an age of specialization. I assume that you, Monsieur LeClerc, are good at what you do. I, at the same time, am a specialist at what I do. Shall we get on with it?"

LeClerc passed the envelope across with another slight shudder.

"Everything you need to know is in here. There is a complete background on the target, as well as photographs and personal habits."

"Current location?"

"It's there, as well as a prediction of any movements in the near future."

"Good," Carter said, slipping the envelope into an inside pocket and lighting another cigarette. "Now, about the remainder of the payment upon completion."

"An additional one hundred thousand dollars upon completion, as agreed. In the envelope there is a Barcelona number to call when the job is done. In light of the quasi-celebrity status of your target, the news media will confirm for us. Within twenty-four hours, the rest of the money will be deposited in your Swiss account."

"Excellent," Carter said. "Now, there is only one more thing. Nels Pomroy."

"What about him?"

"I think I should know a little more about his situation."

"I told you. We think he is dead. Why do you ask?"

"Because I think he may have sold me out somehow. Not informing me of this, for instance." Carter patted the pocket where the envelope rested.

"Quite possible," LeClerc replied, a wan smile accenting his words. "We feel he may have done the same to us."

"How so?"

"I cannot and will not be specific, *monsieur*. As you have said, you are a specialist. We require your services. Beyond that, our business is none of your business. But I can tell you this. Our organization—"

"Which is . . . ?"

"Also none of your business. Our organization has had a slight rift in leadership—"

"So one wants to get rid of the other," Carter interjected.

"Sadly, that is the case. We thought that Monsieur Pomroy was working exclusively for our side in this little power struggle. It would seem that, in point of fact, his allegiance was for the other side and he was only baiting us, draining our funds, and probably reporting our activities to the other side."

Little pinpricks of warning rippled up Carter's spine to lodge under the hair on the back of his neck.

"Then there is a good chance that the target knows I'm coming."

"Yes. But then, *monsieur*, you have stated that you are a specialist."

"True, Monsieur LeClerc. *Touché*."

"Then you will still take the contract?" LeClerc sighed.

"Yes, the challenge intrigues me. But I may need some additional aid: equipment, perhaps some surveillance, and help in escaping when the work is done."

"The Barcelona number can provide you with whatever you need. But I must warn you—my people cannot be actively involved in the kill itself. It would be, shall we say, a public relations faux pas within the group. I'm sure you understand."

"Quite," Carter replied and rescued Hugo from the window catch. "The Luger, butt first."

Reluctantly, Wilhelmina was passed through the opening. Carter leathered it, replaced Hugo, and stepped from the car.

"There will be no need for us to meet again, *monsieur*," LeClerc said. "Good hunting."

"*Adieu*," Carter replied and slammed the door.

He kept one eye on the Mercedes and the other on the area as the big car backed around and began to roll down the hill.

The sun was up full-strength now, so he was able to spot the reflections long before he reached his own vehicle. They came from a large group of trees about a quarter of a mile to his left and a greater elevation of about three hundred yards.

Once, in the limousine, he thought he had seen them. Now, walking across the open area toward the little convertible, they were unmistakably following him.

At the car, in full view of whoever was manning the field glasses, Carter dropped the top and slid behind the wheel.

He drove slowly all the way back to the hotel, not wanting to lose whoever was interested in him.

By the time he had deposited the car and strolled into the lobby, it was fairly clear that both sides of LeClerc's organization knew where he had come after the meeting.

To let them know not only where he was but also *who* he was, he strolled directly to the desk and asked for his key in a loud, clear voice.

"Suite six-eighteen, *s'il vous plaît*."

"Of course, Monsieur Carstocus."

Carter pocketed the key and strolled into the muted warmth of the hotel's wood-paneled restaurant.

"Un menu, s'il vous plaît."

Only when his breakfast had been served and he had requested a second pot of coffee did he remove the envelope from his inside coat pocket.

Slowly he pulled the contents upward from the flap as his eyes searched for the name.

And then he found it.

The target was Armanda de Nerro.

NINE

Carter crossed the frontier into Andorra on the French side at Pas-de-la-Casa. Here he secured a detailed map of the country and sat down over lunch to study it.

The principality was incredibly tiny, 188 square miles, with no airport and no railway system, and on the one main highway that led from the French to the Spanish frontier, the whole country could be crossed in less than an hour.

But that did not tell the whole story, at least as far as Carter was concerned.

Every inch of Andorra was valleys or mountains. There were hundreds, perhaps thousands, of places where the ground could be excavated and silos constructed to house the missiles.

By one o'clock he was back in the car and climbing toward the center of the country via a mountain road that was constantly turning left or right and, often it seemed, both ways at once.

The scenery was magnificent, even after he passed the snow line and a cloudy haze obscured everything beyond a half mile. From the tiny ski village of Soldeu, the terrain flattened out through a place called Ronsol. There he descended downward out of the snow and shut the heater off after only a few miles.

By the time he passed the third largest village, Encamp, and was nearing the capital of Andorra-la-Vella, Carter had gained one very solid impression of the country.

Andorra might once have been a mountain paradise for a small population of farmers and sheep herders, a simple alpine aerie remote from the rest of the world and its troubles.

But no more. Word of its tax-free status had obviously spread, and the world was now beating a track to this tiny country.

The whole face of Andorra was changing, almost hourly. There were workmen, cranes, bulldozers, huge earthmovers, and piles of building materials everywhere.

With all this as cover, it would be no trick at all to build a structure or structures to house eight missiles right under anyone's nose.

In the center of the capital he paused to study the map that Pallmar had given him in Paris as a guide to the villa.

"*Pardon, monsieur*. May I be of help?" a perky female voice asked in French.

She was cute, in a blue and white uniform with a beret perched saucily on a well-coiffed mane of red hair. Above a very prominent left breast was a badge, and in one hand she carried a traffic baton.

"Yes," Carter replied with a jaunty air in his voice. "You can tell me how I can find this villa and then tell me your name."

"The villa, *monsieur,* is easy. Take the road to your right, there, where it says Engordany. The first road you come to, turn right again and go to the end. There you will find the villa. It is a very beautiful house overlooking all of the city. You are a guest of the Englishman, Harris-White?"

"No, I'm leasing the villa for a while. You know the gentleman?"

"No, but it is a small country," she said with a pretty smile. "A person as rich as Monsieur Harris-White who lives in so grand a villa is known by everyone. Enjoy your stay in my country, *monsieur*."

"Wait. You haven't answered my second question."

"Your second question?"

"Your name."

"Marie."

"I am Nicholas Carstocus," he announced. "Now that we have been formally introduced, you can have dinner with me tonight."

"I cannot discuss such things while I am on duty."

"Then what time do you get off duty?"

She glanced quickly to her right and left, and when she spoke again it was with a pixyish grin and a low voice.

"I usually have a glass of wine at the Hotel Roc Blanc lounge on my way home from work at five."

"Five it is, *mademoiselle*," Carter said and waved as he whirled the powerful little car up the street she had indicated.

Harris-White's villa had been built right into the side of a mountain. It was surrounded on three sides by trees, and a gatehouse abutted the dead-end road.

The gate was open. Carter sailed through it and stopped at the steps leading up to a massive, copper-studded oak door.

Almost before he had switched off the ignition, a white-gloved hand was opening the door.

"Señor Carstocus?"

"*Sí*," Carter replied, uncoiling from the sports car.

"I am Robere, the houseboy."

He was a full two feet shorter than Carter, with an almost feminine body, but his smile seemed to go from ear to ear when he grinned.

"The bags are in the trunk. Can you handle them?"

"Of course," Robere said with a shrug, then flashed another grin. "I only look like a girl."

Carter was just reaching for the front door when it opened
wide. A small, dark-haired woman with a gnarled face and
flat, expressionless eyes faced him.

"Señor Carstocus?"

"*Sí.*"

"I am Estrellita, the housekeeper and cook. I do not work
on Saturdays or Sundays, or beyond six o'clock unless I am
paid extra and am warned the previous day. The master suite
is the second door beyond the head of the stairs. What do you
wish for supper?"

"I'll be dining out."

"Good. Welcome to the *casa.*"

She turned and stomped away on stumpy heels.

Truly, Carter thought, *a woman of few words, and one who
knows her own mind.*

He used the time until four o'clock to unpack and
familiarize himself with the house and grounds.

At four he showered and changed into a light short-sleeved
shirt, beige trousers to match, and a cardigan with a de-
signer's name discreetly stitched onto the left breast.

It was a pity, he thought, climbing into the Mercedes, that
Carstocus's taste did not match his own. The wardrobe he
had purchased to match the identity was high-quality stuff.
He could have used it when the mission was over, but as Nick
Carter he hated to be a walking billboard for someone else.

The Hotel Roc Blanc was easy to find. It was located in the
center of the village of Les Escaldes and constructed almost
entirely of white stone quarried from the mountain behind it.

At five after five he walked into the hotel lounge.

Marie sat at a window table sipping a glass of wine. She
had changed into a pair of white wool slacks, a sheer blouse,
and a very form-fitting white sleeveless sweater.

"You don't look anything like a policeperson."

"I'm not a policeperson . . . after five."

"What are you then?"

"My own person."

Carter grinned. "You started without me," he said, nodding toward the wine.

"Yes, but I didn't pay the check."

He laughed and slipped into the chair opposite her. "I think I'm going to like you, Marie . . ."

"Follett."

"Spanish or French?"

"Neither . . . Andorran."

"Good! You should prove to be the perfect guide! I want to see all of Andorra, every mountaintop, every valley. I want to see every building being built and I want to know who is building it."

"Why?"

"I'm thinking of moving here. I like to know my neighbors."

"That could take some time . . ."

"I have a lot of it," Carter replied.

"I have to work in the daytime, I'm afraid."

"Don't you have any vacation time coming?"

"Yes, but . . ."

"I pay my guides quite well."

The following days were spent with Marie, either in the Mercedes or a rented jeep. Carter explored every inch of the country, making his own maps and compiling a long list of the contractors and builders on every piece of construction.

By night he pub-crawled, giving everyone he met the impression that he was a very rich, oversexed roué.

There was an English schoolteacher on vacation and there was a young Spanish widow who had moved to Andorra because she could do things there she could not do in her small provincial hometown. There was the daughter of a French restaurateur who adored handsome, wealthy Greeks, and there was the bored wife of an American banker who lived in Andorra, had most of his business interests in Andorra, but traveled ninety percent of the time.

At the end of a week Carter had enough information to clog a computer, and he had gone through enough women that to seduce one more would hardly be noticed.

It was time to make contact with Louisa Juaneda.

Cabaret Amour was the kind of place that used the silhouette of a nude female for its advertising logo. Alongside the nude, the signs made big promises: DELIGHTFUL LADY COMPANIONS, AMBIANCE AS YOU LIKE IT, SEX ATTRACTIONS NUDE.

And in the Bar Américain there was dancing and the vocal stylings of Louisa Juaneda.

As in any cabaret, the action began after dark . . . *long* after dark. After yet another hard day of tromping the hills with Marie, taking pictures of almost-finished, half-finished, and barely started houses and buildings, Carter slept until nine.

After a shower and a fresh shave, he dressed in gray slacks, a navy jacket, a pale shirt, and a bright red ascot. He had a light supper in one of the better hotel restaurants and walked into the Cabaret Amour at eleven o'clock.

Things were just getting under way.

There was an old woman with the white face of a robot collecting a cover charge and a burly bouncer at the door who informed everyone that at the first inkling of a fight he would break bones no matter who was the instigator.

Carter went down a flight of steps to a cement corridor that smelled of damp concrete. This led through a beaded curtain to the club itself.

Like all European late-night spots, it had the atmosphere of a cave. There were dim lights positioned over tiny tables crowded close together and couples dancing to a disco beat on a small dance floor with rainbow lights bouncing up their pants legs and skirts.

A tall, languorous-looking brunette with most of her anatomy spilling out of a halter top ambled toward him. She would have almost looked erotic if her eyes could focus and she hadn't been chewing gum. ·

"Just you, *monsieur?*"

"*Oui.*"

"A table or the bar? A table is a two-drink minimum."

"I'll take a table. I might scare up some company."

She smiled flatly. "That won't be any trouble in here. Follow me!"

Carter ordered scotch, lit a cigarette, and let his eyes adjust to the gloom.

They made it by the time the scotch arrived.

"What time does the first show start in the Bar Américain?"

"The nude lesbian show or the singer?"

"Uh, the singer," Carter replied, trying to keep a straight face.

"Midnight. It's a two-drink minimum in there, too, but don't worry about it. You'll never get drunk on this stuff."

She was right. The scotch was lousy.

So was the decor, now that Carter could see it. The walls and ceiling were poor rip-offs of the sleazy decor you see in Pigalle clubs in Paris. It was a fair try but lacked the smoky, sultry aura of sin that seemed so much a part of Pigalle.

Here the sin seemed make-believe, even if the customers were trying hard to make it real.

At the table beside Carter, a man of about twenty was sitting hunched across the table, his forehead pressed hard against the forehead of his date. She was a pretty, plump blonde who kept her eyes closed and her fingers curling through his thick black hair.

The man had his hands under the blonde's blouse, kneading with almost dreamlike slowness the full roundness of her breasts where they rested on the table.

At the table beyond them were three girls, all about twenty, and all looking fearfully around the room. Carter guessed the fear was twofold. One, would they be asked to dance or would anyone buy them a drink? Two, what the hell would they do if someone did?

Behind him Carter heard a high-pitched male laugh, and he turned casually.

The table was full of nubile teenage girls and barely bearded boys. One of the girls was wearing an off-the-shoulder dress that had been pulled down low enough to expose a starkly white, darkly nippled breast.

The boy beside her—a hairy cross between modern punk and early Elvis in black leather—was having one hell of a time autographing the breast with a marking pencil.

Everybody at the table—including the girl being autographed—thought the whole thing was a laugh riot.

Suddenly Carter felt very old and oddly puritan.

"Want your other drink?"

"No, thanks. I think I'll hit the other room. Is the crowd any older in there?"

"Yeah, they come to see the singer strip and the lesbians."

That, thought Carter had not been in Louisa Juaneda's résumé.

It took several minutes to wind his way to the blinking sign that announced the Bar Américain. Beneath it was another beaded curtain, and beyond that another burly bouncer.

"Fifty francs cover."

Carter passed over the money.

"There's also a two-drink minimum."

"I heard. Are you sure I'm not in New York?"

"Huh?"

"Nothing."

He found a table right on top of the tiny stage and blinked several times when the waitress arrived. She was a clone of the brunette in the other room.

"Whiskey . . . no water. Make it a double."

She was back in two minutes. The room was not very crowded.

He didn't have long to wait. Three musicians dressed like poorer class bullfighters came through a curtain at the rear of the stage and tuned up.

It didn't take long.

Then a woman's voice, made raspy by too many cigarettes and too much booze, slid through the speakers over the stage.

"Monsieurs et mesdames, the Cabaret Amour is proud to present, directly from Madrid, Barcelona, and Paris, recording star Louisa Juaneda . . ."

There was a smattering of applause as the lights dimmed. An amber spot flickered on and danced around the room until it found the curtain at the rear of the stage.

When it did, a vision in silver sequins stepped through and glided like a cat to a stool before the microphone. Once there, she draped herself over the stool and lifted the mike from its cradle.

The outfit, a floor-length skirt and tiny halter, was something to behold. What it held was breathtaking.

Louisa Juaneda was breathtaking.

The band, muted and surprisingly good, came in behind her in perfect synchronization to her low, throaty, almost raspy voice. She literally oozed through three slow ballads, each greeted with perfunctory applause.

Carter could see why. She was no singer. Her voice, while sultry and somewhat alluring, was weak and almost void of range.

But somehow she seemed to pull it off. As he watched and listened, he began to understand why. It was a combination of her eyes, deep and almond-shaped, the satin black sheen of her carefully coiffed hair arranged in a long swirl over her right shoulder, her tanned skin, and her voluptuous figure compressed just so in the sequined costume.

Then the tempo of the music changed. It was still low-key with an aura of smoldering sex, but now the beat seemed to take over and the rhythm became more driving.

And Louisa Juaneda began to move.

It did not take Carter long to realize that this was what made her act a success.

The voice became more strident, matching the movements of her perfectly coordinated body. All at the same time, she had that rarest of qualities: the beauty and effervescence of youth plus the experience of age. She was, Carter knew, around thirty. But now, as she slithered back and forth across the tiny stage, she seemed barely twenty: young, tender, and sexy.

The lights narrowed down to just the spot on her. The orchestra was little more than a driving bass beat.

Slowly, sensually, she leaned far back, her upper torso disappearing beneath hips that arched upward toward the ceiling. Her thighs corded tautly, and suddenly she was upright again, moving like a cat.

The halter was gone, and her large, coned breasts jutted their darkly coraled nipples toward the light.

This time there was real applause and gasps of approval from the crowd.

Her free hand did things to her hair and suddenly it became uncoiled. It billowed down her back, over her shoulders, and caressed her dancing breasts without obscuring them.

As the song reached a crescendo, her eyes narrowed to slits. The words of the song from her throat became little more than orgasmic groans.

Suddenly, with only a wriggle of her hips, the skirt fell away to puddle on the floor at her feet.

Completely naked, she hit the last note and the spotlight blinked out.

Applause rolled to the stage, and the light came back on.

Incredibly, in those few seconds, she had somehow managed to get the skirt and halter back in place.

She took two quick bows and was gone.

"*Merci, merci, monsieurs et mesdames,*" said the whiskey-voiced woman over the speakers. "The next show will be in one hour . . . the Daughters of Aphrodite!"

Carter lifted his glass above his head and waved it until the brunette waitress noticed him. While he waited for the drink, he jotted a message in his notebook, ripped out the page, and wrapped it in a twenty-franc note.

"Would you give this to Señorita Juaneda, *por favor*?"

"*Sí, señor.*"

Carter watched her amble away, her hips imitating a metronome.

Five minutes later he placed a cigarette between his lips and a lighter flared in front of its tip. A slim brown hand moved the lighter to the cigarette. Carter inhaled and plumed the smoke from his nostrils as he turned toward her.

The hair now hung in sleek lines framing her face. She wore a baggy turtleneck minidress that came just below her hips and black mesh stockings on her legs.

She looked very Parisian, and, if Carter hadn't known better, he would have taken her for just another teenager in the bar.

"Señor Carstocus?"

"I adored your act . . . especially the ending."

"Thank you. You wish to buy me a drink?"

"A great many drinks. Please sit down."

She sat and lit her own cigarette. It was barely going before the brunette waitress set a glass of wine beside her hand.

"You are Greek?"

"No, American, but I have been living in Paris."

"Your Spanish is very good."

"Thank you."

"How long have you been in Andorra?" she asked, her face sporting a wide smile that revealed perfect white teeth.

"Just a week," he replied, ignoring the beautiful bones of her face, the sleek hair, and the fleshy perfection of her body that even the baggy dress failed to hide.

Instead he concentrated on those dark, almond eyes. They were intense, penetrating, and very communicative.

"On holiday?"

"No, I'm looking for a building site. I may decide to move here."

It was almost imperceptible, but Carter noticed the tenseness leave her shoulders now that the contact had been firmly established.

They chatted inanely until the headline show was announced, and Carter suggested they taste the delights of a few of the other late-night spots.

"You're sure you don't want to see the Daughters of Aphrodite in action?" she asked with a sly smile.

Carter shrugged and returned her smile. "I think you are much more interesting."

Just as they were going through the beaded curtain, he saw the brunette who had waited on him mount the stage. And then he saw her clone from the other room get up beside her.

My God, he thought, they *were* clones: twins.

"You mean they really . . . ?"

"Yes," Louisa said, nodding. "Isn't it amazing what people will pay to watch?"

She was good.

They hit four spots, had a drink in each one, and at no time was business ever mentioned. Indeed, the conversation never got above the level of inane chatter, mainly directed toward feeling each other out concerning where they would eventually spend the night together.

In each place, they got more cozy. Little touches and looks got more intimate. When they left the last club, they walked arm in arm to the Mercedes.

Carter opened the passenger side door. He was about to hand Louisa in, when she turned into his arms.

"Kiss me!"

As their lips met she slid his hands around her waist and then pushed them down to the supple arcs of her buttocks. At the same time, she moved against him. Once there, she started grinding.

At last, with sweat trickling down Carter's back, she broke the embrace and moved her lips to his ear.

"That should assure them that all you've done tonight is make another conquest."

"Yeah, I would think so," he rasped, closing the door behind her and moving to the driver's side.

They were through Andorra-la-Vella and making the turn up toward the villa before she relaxed and spoke.

"They've made you."

"They were supposed to," he replied, skillfully maneuvering the little car on the upward curves without braking. "The question is, which side. How much do you know?"

"Everything I had to, prior to your leaving Paris."

Her demeanor had changed completely now. She was still sexy, but without the come-hither coquettishness. The sexiness now just came naturally with her, and the rest was all business.

Carter briefed her about Marseille, about Marc LeClerc, and explained in detail what he had meant about the two sides.

"That's a twist. Then the ones who have been watching you could be on Armanda de Nerro's side, *or* LeClerc's."

"If LeClerc is more than just a banker. I don't think so."

"Then there's someone—a rival leader in the ETA—who

wants to get rid of de Nerro and take over.''

Carter nodded. "And I think whoever it is wants to take the whole scam over, missiles and all.''

"What about the try on this moderate, Julio Mendez, in Pakolo?''

"My guess is that de Nerro was behind that as well. She wants all her opposition in the movement, moderate and radical, out of the way. What have you found out about her since you've been here?''

"Not much," Louisa replied with a slight shake of her head. "She's very social, worked her way into what society there is here. She has a suite in Andorra's deluxe hotel, The Park, with her mother. She rarely goes out in public, usually only attends very private parties given by the very wealthy.''

"Have you made the party or parties that have been watching me?''

"A few of them, but I couldn't tell you if they were hers or not. Also, I haven't been keeping tabs on her too closely. I was only set up here to help you and back you up if you needed it.''

"That's okay. I've got a list of every building under construction and every excavation being made in the country. Can you get the list to Madrid for me and check out everyone connected?''

Louisa nodded. "I'll go to Barcelona in the morning for new costumes. It's routine, once a week. I'll get it to Madrid from there.''

"Good. Have them put a rush on it! Here we are.''

Carter stopped at the villa's steps, cut the lights and motor, and moved around to open the door for her.

"Get loving," she whispered as they moved to the steps.

He did, squeezing her with one arm while he fumbled for the right key with the hand of the other.

"Have you checked the house for bugs?" she asked.

"Only the upstairs. It's clean.''

"Which bedroom are you using?"

"Master suite, second door on the right, head of the stairs."

"I'll go on up," she said, then raised her voice as the door swung inward. "What a beautiful villa! I so adore wealth and the good life, *señor*. Don't be long!"

Carter watched her bouncy bottom go up the stairs until it was out of sight. Then he went through the house, checking door locks and killing lights.

In the den he grabbed a bottle of calvados and two glasses.

"I thought you might like a glass of bran—"

Louisa stood, bathed in light, directly in front of the three bay windows that faced down the mountain to the road and Andorra-la-Vella beyond.

Slowly, sensuously, she was pulling the baggy dress up her body.

Carter rocked to a halt and finally settled on his heels.

"If they're watching, which I'm sure they are," she said, "we had better keep your reputation—and my cover—intact."

"Yeah," Carter gulped. "Good idea."

He watched, fascinated, as the dress rose an inch at a time.

As the hem climbed. Carter's interest and fascination soared with it. He had already seen her nude once that night, but now there was an added erotic stimulus: they were alone, together, in a bedroom.

She was turned just so, the main thrust of the strip being directed to the unseen viewer outside the window. But there was enough front—and more than enough profile—so that Carter also got the full effect of the show.

The dress was halfway off now, revealing lushly flared hips, insolently arched buttocks. Her belly was sleek, faintly rounded, punctuated saucily by the dimple of her navel. On up over the slim column of her waist the dress went. It was a tiny waist that accentuated the spectacular curve of her hips.

Then Carter felt a vein begin to throb in his temple as the fleshy spheres of her breasts came into view. As heavy as they were, they sat high on her chest. They were ripely rounded, and in this light Carter could see that the areolas were almost brown.

Casually, Louisa dropped the dress and deftly slithered out of the black panties Carter had barely noticed.

Then, completely nude, she shook her hair loose over her shoulders the way television models do to demonstrate their newly shampooed manes.

Carter almost dropped the bottle and glasses.

"There, that should do it."

"Yeah," he replied hoarsely, "it sure as hell should."

Pertly she waltzed to the bed, threw back the covers, and slid between them. When she was covered to her chin, she looked up at him questioningly.

"Well?"

"I'm not sure."

"I mean," she chuckled, "you can turn out the light now and come to bed. I'm sure they've seen enough to convince them that I'm just another of your dalliances."

"Yeah," he replied dryly, hitting the wall switch and plunging the room into darkness, "I'm sure they have."

Awkwardly he managed to divest himself of his clothing, then he slid into the bed beside her.

"Did you bring the brandy?"

"What? . . . Oh, sure."

He poured two glasses and found her groping hand with one of them in the darkness.

He did not know what he had expected, but it turned out to still be business.

"I'll take the list to Barcelona tomorrow," she said matter-of-factly. "What else can I be working on for you until we get the feedback?"

Her scent was assaulting his nostrils, and her warmth had

already invaded the bed. It was a hard task, but he finally managed to formulate and voice an answer.

"Do you have any contacts in town who would know when de Nerro will be attending the next society bash?"

"Two, maybe three. Her maid has the apartment across from mine. We sometimes have tea together. I've also gotten to know Jock Loran. He comes to the club. He's usually her escort to the parties. Also, we have our hair done at the same place. De Nerro is a regular. It's a good chance that her hairdresser would know if she's having a hairdo for a special occasion."

"Perfect. Also, the chances are pretty good that the missiles have already entered the country. But wherever they are to be housed is probably under construction. That means the architect, Adam Greenspan, and the engineer, Lorenzo Montegra, will already be here getting things set up. The two of them will have to be housed under guard somewhere."

"It could be anywhere."

"Yeah, it could," Carter replied. "But the domestic underground—waiters, drivers, bartenders, etc.—get wind of things like that."

"I'll see what I can do." There was a pause. Carter heard her sip the brandy and then set the glass on the floor beside the bed. "If de Nerro knows you are the one LeClerc sent, she might try for you first."

"She hasn't in the week I've been here, but you're right . . . she might."

"What will you do?"

"Get them before they get me."

"I see." Another pause. "Anything else?"

"That's it."

"All right. Good night."

"Good night?"

"You said that was it."

"Yeah," Carter replied, downing the remains in the

brandy glass. "Yeah, I did, didn't I?"

He heard her turn on her side, and almost at once her breathing was even.

He thought of the recent night in the Marseille hotel room with Lily, and sighed.

Odd, he thought, *this overpowering attraction I have for sexless one-night stands. . . .*

TEN

He started out life as Alan Smith from Pittsburgh. But now he was Alain Smythe of London, *haute coutourier* to any woman who could pay his price.

It was his party, a housewarming to celebrate his new-found freedom from English taxes. He had taken a large, medieval stone castle and completely renovated it. The exterior was made up of sprawling, crenelated walls, turrets, round, soaring towers, and even a workable drawbridge over a wide, deep moat.

The interior was exactly the opposite, with decor that would grace a Parisian townhouse. He had all the modern accouterments, including Olympic-size bathtubs and a kitchen that sported a microwave oven alongside an old-style open pit that would accommodate an entire boar for roasting.

Smythe had been slumming at the Cabaret Amour one evening with his companion and secretary, Charles, and had caught Louisa's act.

"Brava, my dear, truly decadent. I'm having a little soiree to announce myself to the rest of the expatriate community and christen the renovation of my new abode. I would be charmed if you would attend and . . . perhaps perform."

"I would be glad to, *señor,*" Louisa had coyly replied.

"May I bring a friend?"

"Male or female?"

"Male."

"Most assuredly. Sunday next."

It was cocktails at eight, dinner at ten. Carter and Louisa had arrived at eight-thirty. They were the first ones there.

Now it was nine, and the great room of Alain Smythe's home-cum-castle was teeming with the beautiful people. Carter had already spotted two of his former conquests and nimbly countered their propositions for a rematch.

At nine-fifteen, Armanda de Nerro made her appearance on the arm of a young, blond-haired Greek god. Carter guessed this was the Jock Loran that Louisa had mentioned as being her usual escort to these functions.

Armanda was everything her pictures portrayed, and more. She was pure class, tall, with the kind of legs that go all the way up.

She wore a skintight piece of velvet for a dress that dipped clear to her navel in front. The absence of a bra let everyone in the room, who cared, know that she was very real under the velvet. The hair, if possible, was even blacker than Louisa's, with brief flashes of red shining in just the right light. It fell to the gentle slopes of her derrière in the back and across her shoulders in the front to drape suggestively across the slope of her breasts.

Carter met her eyes the second she walked into the room and thought that, just before she turned away, there was the briefest flash of recognition.

Good enough, he thought. *You know me, I know you. Now let's see how good the first move is and who makes it.*

Alain Smythe met Armanda the moment she hit the room. He kissed her hand and said something charming—and probably obscene—to her young escort.

De Nerro, in the true tradition of beautiful people, threw

her head back in a lusty laugh. Her teeth were perfect and her throat was shapely. To Carter it looked as kissable as the rest of her.

Carter's attention shifted to Jock Loran. He was handsome, almost pretty, in the classic Italian and Spanish way. He moved like a bullfighter, but beneath the tuxedo jacket he had the physique and, Carter suspected, the well-trained, well-honed muscles of a heavyweight boxer.

His face, as well as his body, did not say "playboy." The nose had been broken a couple of times but had been well set. The forehead was low between blond hair, meticulously cut, and bushy golden brows.

But it was the eyes that told Carter that Jock Loran was as much or more bodyguard for Armanda de Nerro than he was escort.

They were like clear blue ice. Carter knew the look in those eyes. He saw the same look every morning in his own when he shaved.

They were the eyes of a killer.

As confirmation to his conclusion was the slight bulge beneath the man's jacket. Carter guessed a Beretta or Luger like his own Wilhelmina.

"I'm sure you've noticed . . . she's here." It was Louisa at his elbow.

"It's hard to miss her," Carter replied.

"I know. God, she is beautiful."

"Not any more than you," Carter replied, his teeth gleaming in a smile. "Just richer. Wealth somehow transmits itself to its owners, making them seem more beautiful."

"My God, he's a philosopher too."

"Only on Sunday evenings. Can you get Loran away from Armanda and Smythe?"

"Shouldn't be too hard," Louisa replied. "He's a man."

The way she said it made Carter think she didn't care too

much for the male population. Maybe, he thought, that was why they had already slept together and there had been no hanky-panky.

Louisa was a cat going across the room, and an eel moving her arm through Loran's and her body against his.

A few words were exchanged, Loran looked at his boss, and Carter saw a barely perceptible nod of de Nerro's beautiful head.

He freshened his drink, waited as long as he dared before someone else busted up their tête-à-tête, and crossed the room.

Carter had engratiated himself with Smythe immediately upon their arrival by assuming as shallow a character as his host.

As subtly as possible, Carter had also let the man know that he was not just attracted to beautiful women.

God, he thought, *the poses one must assume now and then for the good of one's country!*

"Alain, the renovation is marvelous, the interior is divine. I can't wait to see the rest of the place!" he gushed.

"Oh, thank you, dear boy. Perhaps after we dine I can give you the grand tour . . . *personally.*"

There was a gleam in the little man's eye that made Carter very uncomfortable. He struggled not to show it.

"Oh, allow me to introduce you to Armanda de Nerro. Armanda, Nicholas Carstocus."

"How do you do, *señor*?"

"Charmed, *mademoiselle.*"

Any Prussian count would have been proud of Carter's style. The bow was precise, the heels almost clicked, the acceptance of the proffered hand was suave, and the kiss was cosmopolitan.

"Nicholas, like all of us," Smythe declared, "is a refugee from taxes. American, very rich, and, as you can see, Armanda, very handsome.'' Here one of the bright eyes in the pasty little face blinked. ''Just *your* type, Armanda.''

''Oh, really, Alain, how amusing you are.'' She turned her eyes toward Carter, and there was everything in them but amusement. ''My apologies, Señor Carstocus.''

''Oh? What for?''

''When I first arrived, I thought you were some kind of very rugged detective or security person that Alain had hired to protect the guests' jewels.''

The sting in her tone let Carter know in no uncertain terms that she knew the man behind the facade.

He played off of it. He laughed.

''I'm afraid I could never be a detective. I've heard it's a boring occupation. And as far as guarding jewels, I would much rather steal them.''

''Appearances can be deceiving,'' she countered.

''Aren't they though?''

About that time, a chorus at the bar started screeching for Smythe. With a bright ''Excuse me'' and a little wave, Smythe was gone.

De Nerro made small talk. As Carter matched it, he studied her face. It was classic, much more so than her photographs, with all the points fine. But it was her mouth that drew his attention. It was wide, with full, sensuous, kissable lips.

He wondered if those lips could be as cruel as they were sensuous.

At last he said, ''You're Spanish?''

''Basque.''

''Is there a difference?''

The eyes narrowed. ''A very large difference.''

''Really?'' Carter replied, all innocence. ''I'm afraid I'm not very versed on—''

''Dance with me,'' she interrupted, gliding into his arms.

''What?''

"Dance with me. Someone is coming that I do not want to talk to."

Her body was firm and soft all at the same time. The smile on her dark face was enigmatic. It teased and taunted, and yet it seemed to invite. He decided to make his pitch, but she spoke again before he got the chance.

"Don't you find these parties boring?"

"Not always. Sometimes you meet the most interesting people . . . like you, for instance." Carter grinned. "Are you attached to the blond man . . . the one you arrived with?"

"I am attached to no one," Armanda said curtly.

Carter decided it was now or never. "Then, since you find the party boring and you're not attached to your escort, would you like to go somewhere else . . . my villa, for instance . . . and do something?"

"What, for instance?"

Carter shrugged. "Go to bed," he said with a straight face.

Her answering laugh was low and throaty and totally genuine. "You are blunt, to say the least."

Her body relaxed, melted against his. She was provoking him, pasting her thighs to his and twisting her hips. Carter tried to release her, but she held him by the waist and drew him in closer. Her breasts pillowed across his chest, and for a moment he thought they would escape the dress.

"You still haven't answered my question," he murmured.

"It sounds like fun," she said, a tone of manufactured lust in her voice. "But I am afraid I shall be busy until very late this evening."

"Tomorrow evening then . . . I'm planning a small, intimate dinner party."

"At your villa?"

"Yes, the Harris-White place. You know it?"

"I know it. What time?"

"A decent hour. Shall we say nine?"

"Nine it is, Señor Carstocus."

She slipped from his arms as quickly and deftly as she had entered them, leaving Carter standing in the center of the floor.

He watched her move into an adjoining room and up a flight of stairs. In her wake was Alain Smythe. Carter was about to follow, when a powerful, heavily muscled arm moved around his shoulders.

It was Jock Loran.

"Señor Carstocus, Señorita Juaneda is about to sing in the salon. I know you don't want to miss it."

The steady, penetrating look in the man's eyes and the viselike grip on his shoulder told Carter that if he did want to miss it, he would have to break Loran's arm to do so.

Carter had little doubt that he could accomplish that, but it would prove nothing.

He decided to let it rest for this evening and learn what he could the next.

It was three in the morning when he dropped Louisa off at her hotel. By the time he reached the road leading up to the villa, it had started snowing lightly.

The car skidded slightly as he drove through the gates, but he was able to right it and glide the rest of the way to the front door.

He was three paces from the steps, fumbling for the right key, when it hit him.

He had closed and locked the gates when he had left.

They came, six strong . . . three from the bushes to his right, three more running headlong from the bushes to his left.

Carter bolted backward and rolled just in time to avoid a body block from a big, beefy, football type. At the same time, he clawed for Wilhelmina in the holster above his boot.

He got the Luger out, but before he could put her to any use, one of the three from the trees put a shoulder square into his back.

The Luger skittered from Carter's hand, and he heard it slide over the drive as the force of the hit sent him sprawling over the rear section of the Mercedes.

He went with it, rolled, and came up ready.

Two of them came at him at once, with a third close behind in the center. Carter got a chop in with his right hand. While he was distracted, his left arm was pulled and squeezed at the nerve just above the elbow.

They were good.

The numbing in his left arm was instantaneous, from his shoulder to the tips of his fingers.

He tried to break the hold with his right, only to have it grabbed with the same intent.

"If we wanted you dead, Carstocus, you would be dead."

It was the big, beefy one. He stood directly in front of Carter, waiting to pounce.

"So what do you want me to do? Lie down and *play* dead?"

"Something like that," the man replied. "Or I use this."

A long hypodermic gleamed in his right hand.

Carter shrugged and relaxed in his captor's grip.

"That's more like it."

He was two feet in front of Carter when the Killmaster used his own hands to grip the wrists of the arms that held him. Using them as leverage, he drop-kicked the one in front of him directly in the crotch.

The man had barely hit the ground when Carter freed his right arm. He swung his weight, wrapping his free arm around the neck of the one still holding him. Then, using one body as a fulcrum, he planted his boot heels in the face of the other.

When his feet hit the ground, he continued the fall, got his shoulder in the guy's gut, and lifted.

Up he went and down he came, right across the top of the Mercedes. He heard bones break in tandem with the shredding canvas.

Carter whirled, but in an instant he could see it was too late. The other three were all over him.

He managed to nail one in the kneecap with his toe and tried to sidestep the other two.

It was useless.

They both hit him at once from the sides, one high, one low.

As he went down under the superior weight, Carter tried to get a thumb into an eye, but an elbow came down hard into his gut.

Then he was beneath them, flat out on the drive, and they were both working on his guts with fists that felt like lead weights.

He did his best to keep from passing out, but it was a losing proposition.

The last thing Carter heard was a guttural, growling voice rasping, ''Goddamnit, don't kill him and don't mark him up!''

He was completely out for only about three minutes, but it took a good half hour to become fully cognizant and breathe normally.

Carter opened one eye to a slit but stayed slumped in the seat.

He was between two of them in the back seat of a sedan. Two more were in the front seat, and through the windshield he could see the other two in his own Mercedes.

The snow was heavy now, but through it he could see that they were on a narrow mountain road. As they drove, Carter tried to nail a few landmarks.

He could not, which made him think they had somehow crossed the border into Spain.

Why Spain?

Because, since being in Andorra, Carter had navigated and cased every drivable road—and some that had not been drivable—in the entire country.

He could not spot one familiar piece of terrain or recognize any of the little villages or gas stations they passed. Other than the two frontier crossings on the main highway, there was a small, little-used road leading west into the Spanish Pyrenees from Andorra.

It was mostly used by farmers bringing their market goods into Andorra and led nowhere in Spain except to a few small villages.

If they wanted to get a beat-up, passed-out man out of Andorra for a while, that was the road they would use.

Ergo, Carter surmised, he was in Spain . . . and close to Basque country.

Had Armanda de Nerro decided to jump the gun and simply do away with him before she could use her body to interrogate him?

Could be, he thought, but there was not much he could do about it at this point.

They came down off a mountain in a long, arcing valley. At the bottom Carter could see scattered lights. The road near the bottom got bumpier and, as they neared a village, was not maintained at all.

Both cars slowed, and up ahead Carter saw an unlit sign: La Siesta.

It could have been a pre-World War II cabin court just

across the border from San Diego in Tijuana.

Both cars lurched over a gutted cement apron and moved between two long rows of tin-roofed, paintless cabins that looked more like livestock sheds with tattered curtains at their windows.

Where there wasn't a shack there were mounds of garbage, scrub trees, and discarded parts of ancient automobiles. Here the snow seemed to turn black or brown the instant it hit the ground, making it resemble a patchwork carpet . . . or a garbage collage done by a mad artist.

"Nice place," Carter groaned to let them know he was awake. "Early sleaze."

Right and left glanced at him, but neither of them said a word.

They came to a halt beside the last building in the line. It was larger than the rest, double width, and, unlike several of the others, no light came through the windows.

Carter was just wondering about all the signs of wakefulness at this hour of the morning, when the door of the shanty directly across from them opened and two men stepped out. Directly behind came two women.

With the amount of makeup, the hairstyles, and the clothing he could see in the opening of their coats, it didn't take a student of the streets to figure out the action.

The place was either a brothel or a motel-by-the-hour where the girls took their tricks.

They sat in the silent car until the two men and women had driven away. Then the door opened and Carter was yanked from the car.

One held his arms behind him while the other—the big, beefy one he had tried to make a soprano out of—leaned his face close.

"I cannot kill you, *señor,* but if you make one sudden move, here or inside, you will need new kidneys."

He held up one broad fist. There was a sock wrapped around the fingers, and Carter guessed it was filled with coins.

Carter nodded his understanding.

About three good blows in the small of the back with that, and he knew he would need a transplant if he ever wanted to pee properly again.

"Around back!"

They formed a wedge around him, with the beefy one directly behind, and moved him along.

Inside was a bed, a drawerless dresser with a cracked mirror, one chair, and a chipped pan on a stool that was probably supposed to be used as a chamber pot. Other than a crucifix over the bed, there was nothing else on the bare floor and peeling walls.

A candle beside the chamber pot gave the only illumination.

A door in the wall was open to darkness. Carter guessed it was an adjoining room, the reason why the shack looked twice as big as the others.

Carter was hustled to a chair facing the black opening and shoved down. His butt had barely hit, when a powerful flashlight was snapped on and directly into his eyes.

He tried to turn his head, only to have a hand come out from behind the flash and bring him forward with an open-handed slap.

"Señor Carstocus, my patience is very nearly at an end."

Carter smiled and worked his jaw back and forth a few times before replying. "I don't really give a damn."

Again the hand, this time the back of it, across the opposite cheek.

"Listen carefully to what I say!"

The language was Spanish, but by now Carter had learned the dialectical quirks of a Basque speaker.

Whoever was playing patty-cake with his face was definitely Basque.

"You've got my attention," Carter said.

"Good. You are Bluebeard, and I am your principal employer."

Carter could not stop the slight element of shock that covered his face. It could still be a gimmicky trick of de Nerro's, but somehow he doubted it.

"We only have forty-eight hours left. Your target must be eliminated by then. I want to know your plans."

"Even if I knew what you were talking about," Carter replied, "I only do business with Pepe."

"Marc LeClerc died in Nice three days ago . . . the victim of a very powerful bomb placed under the rear seat of his car."

Carter hesitated, letting this sink in, and then decided to play ball. "Who did it?"

"My guess is that our lady friend issued the order. Marc was, how you say in America, straddling the fence between Armanda and myself, but he knew of her ambition and treachery. His allegiance was, as it has always been, to me."

"And who are you?"

"That need not concern you, but I have many reasons for wanting that betraying bitch dead. Now, what are your plans?"

Carter tried to get in one more jab. "Why the sudden time limit?"

Again the hand, back and forth several times, until Carter was starting to hear the chimes of Westminster somewhere deep in his skull.

"All right . . . all right. Tomorrow night. I've invited her to the villa for dinner."

"The time?"

"Nine o'clock."

"And after dinner?"

"I will seduce her and drug her."

"A lethal dose of some drug?"

"No. It's called Lysoghin. It can be induced through the pores in the skin and cannot be detected in an autopsy."

"Then how do you plan to make the kill?"

"May I have a cigarette?"

The light wiggled and a cigarette was shoved between his lips. As he drew in the smoke, he dreamed up the next lie.

"An automobile accident on the hairpin turn just beneath the villa."

There was a long silence from the blackness, and then the light snapped off.

"So be it. Just make sure it happens. As I have said, we can wait no longer. Ramos . . . ?"

"Here," came a voice from behind Carter.

"Give him the keys to his car and take him out. Señor Carstocus . . . ?"

"Yes?"

"If Manda is still among the living twenty-four hours from now, you won't be. Get him out of here!"

Carter was yanked to his feet and half carried, half dragged from the cabin. When they reached the Mercedes, the keys were shoved into his hand by the beefy one called Ramos, and the door opened for him.

"I'll need my gun back," Carter said.

"Gun, señor? What gun?"

The man's gaze was steady, unwavering. It was impossible to tell if he was lying or not.

"The Luger you knocked from my hand when you took me."

"If you lost your gun, señor, it is still where you lost it. Get in the car!"

He had no choice.

The powerful engine roared to life, and Carter leaned out the window.

"Ramos?"

"*Si?*"

"I never forget a face."

"So?"

"So, Ramos, the next time I see yours, I'm going to kill you."

ELEVEN

The meal was excellent. Through the courses of delicious, wafer-thin salmon caught in the local waters, chilled gazpacho, endive and avocado salad, and mouth-watering paella, each accompanied by the proper wine, they verbally sparred and parried across the candlelit table.

Carter had dropped his facade of gay raconteur midway through the appetizer. Armanda de Nerro did the same. There was still a bit of the wily courtesan in her physical poses and her manners, but her speech and the intensity in her eyes said much more.

Throughout the meal, the events of the previous evening ran through Carter's mind. All of his suppositions after Pepe and Marseille had pretty well fallen into place. It mattered little who his principal employer was. What was important was that the man had given Carter ammunition to squeeze Armanda de Nerro.

That is, if she could be squeezed.

When the dessert was served, Carter excused Estrellita and told her to inform the rest of the servants that they could leave.

Now he escorted the tall, dark-haired beauty into the music room, its tall bay windows looking out over the blinking lights of Andorra-la-Vella and the snow-shrouded mountains behind.

"More wine? Perhaps a brandy?"

"Brandy, I think."

"Good."

Carter poured two heavy cut-glass goblets half full and passed one to her. As her jeweled fingers curled around the bowl of the goblet, her lips curled in crimson amusement.

"You have as large an appetite for drink as you do for good food, Nicholas."

"True," Carter said, sipping. "I am part Greek, part American, and all barbarian."

"And I've been told that you have an equal appetite for women."

"Also true."

Together, with Carter slightly behind at her shoulder, they moved into one of the bays.

"And am I to be just another of your conquests this evening?"

"I think, dear lady, that is entirely up to you," Carter said with a smile. "But—let me say this—I don't think anyone will ever conquer you."

"A few have tried," she said, rolling her head to the side and moving her shoulder back until their lips almost touched.

"I've heard. Your husbands, for instance. They all came to violent ends."

Again the flat smile, as deadly as it was amused. "You seem to know a great deal about me, Nicholas Carstocus, whereas I know very little about you."

"What would you like to know?"

"Well, for instance . . . what do you do besides host small, intimate dinner parties, drink good wine, and seduce women?"

Carter matched the cold amusement of her smile and used

his eyes to bore through hers into the core of her soul.

"I kill people."

She blinked once, and other than the smile fading, there was no other sign that he had said anything at all out of the ordinary.

"As I noted at Alain's party, you are quite blunt."

"Even more so now. We both know . . . ergo, why fence any longer?"

"When you kill . . . it is for money?"

"Not entirely. There is also the element of risk, the danger involved in hunting the ultimate quarry . . . man."

"Or woman?"

"Or woman."

Carter knew he was getting the better of the cat-and-mouse game, but she hid it well. A hand deftly moving her hair back from her face, a sip of the brandy, a quick glance at him only to roll her eyes back to the twinkling lights before them, all to formulate her next step, her next speech.

When she did speak, she turned first to face him directly. Carter sensed something new, almost predatory in her classic, aristocratic features and full mouth.

"I distrust adventurers, particularly those who place monetary gain as the bedrock of their actions."

Carter shrugged, not moving his eyes from hers. "You're entitled to your opinion. As for myself, I distrust ideologies and those who would blindly pursue them."

"Touché." She seemed to relax, even going so far as to reach out and run a long, ruby-red nail along Carter's cheekbone. "You are a fascinating man and, I understand, quite ingenious."

She moved slightly, just enough to press her cushiony breasts against his chest. The touch was electric, and Carter did not try to hide his reaction.

"I wonder what it would be like to have a man like

you—with your intensity, your total lack of morals, of scruples, an almost *inhuman* human—inside me.''

"There is but one way to find out.''

"When do you plan to kill me, Señor Bluebeard? Before, during, or after?''

"I would never forego the joys of the flesh for money.''

"And how . . . how am I to meet my Maker?''

"I haven't decided yet.''

"Perhaps . . . during . . . I can convert you.''

"Convert me?''

"Yes . . . with the added inducement of money, of course. Say, double what LeClerc offered you?''

"That would be a strong inducement. The master suite is on the right at the top of the stairs.''

Armanda pirouetted and moved as if there were only air beneath her feet across the room and down the wide hall. Carter lit a cigarette and took several drags as he listened to her heels on the carpeted stairs.

When the sound faded, he moved into the great room, extinguishing lights as he went. In the darkness he mounted the stairs and then peered intently out the windows toward the winding road below.

Though the snow was coming down hard now, he could make out their car, a gray sedan. It was parked in a turnout on the first curve just below the villa.

Shielding the glow of his cigarette in his hand, he quickly let the pieces of the rest of the evening fall into place.

Armanda de Nerro was firmly convinced of his identity and the reason for his presence in Andorra.

As a hired killer, he had been bought. Therefore, he could be bought again. The price? Her body and enough dollars.

But, for Carter, that wouldn't be quite enough.

He would have to frighten her just a little bit more. He would have to make sure that his guess was right about the person who wanted her dead and wanted to take control of the ETA organization.

Then he would convince her that he, Nicholas Carstocus, could be of even further help to her. But only if he knew everything.

Once in the lady's confidence, Carter was fairly sure he could get the rest of it before she no longer needed him: mainly, the location of the missiles.

He walked down the stairs again and across the great room. The house was as still as a tomb as he mounted the main staircase and walked into the master suite.

She was the Naked Maja, sprawled beautifully across the bed. She had dimmed the lights until they seemed to make her body glow on the stark white linen sheets.

Carter could see every curve, every hollow, and every dimple in her supple body.

Before leaving, Estrellita had built a small fire. It burned low, providing little heat but a great deal of atmosphere.

Carter let his eyes drink in Armanda's nakedness as he slipped the dinner jacket and then the shirt from his body.

He continued to undress in unison with his movement toward her. His knees were against the foot of the bed when she spoke.

"Who is it, Nicholas?"

"Who?"

"The one who hired you?"

"LeClerc."

"No. LeClerc was only a messenger boy, a liaison. Was it Mendez, that old fool? Did he finally realize that violence is the only way?"

"Is that why you wanted Julio Mendez killed? Because you thought it was he who wanted you dead?"

"How did you know . . . ?"

There wasn't much time now. He could see the wariness in

her eyes, the look of an animal about to spring.

Words, phrases, accents from the previous evening flashed through Carter's brain.

. . . that betraying bitch. . . .

Who had Armanda de Nerro betrayed?

"You do know, don't you," she said, her voice a whisper. "You do. I can see it in your eyes."

"I think I know . . . Manda."

Her hand came from beneath the pillow, holding a small automatic. Like a cat her body rolled from the bed. She was already swinging the gun around as her knees touched the carpet and her body tucked, making herself a spare target.

Carter had expected a reaction, but not one quite this bizarre.

Obviously the one thing she had wanted from Carter was the identity of her rival.

Now that she had it, Carter's usefulness was over.

The sound of the little gun firing was little more than a pop, but the flame shooting from the muzzle was bright in the dim room.

He could feel the slug pass by his ear as he threw himself onto the bed. She was rolling to her right on one knee as he bounced off the mattress above her.

The gun popped again, and Carter felt a tug on his left forearm as his right hand smashed her wrist. She groaned in pain but made a dive for the gun.

Carter managed to push it farther from her grasp with his knee and swung his right arm in a wide, powerful arc. The flat of his hand collided smartly with the side of her face.

She spun crazily across the carpet until her back hit the wall. Carter was on her in a second, but there was still a lot of life left in her.

Both hands whipped toward his face like claws, her razor-like nails digging deep gouges in his cheeks.

Again his hand whipped around. This time the blow was solid. The sound of his knuckles against her chin was like a shot in the otherwise quiet room.

Armanda started to fold as he grabbed her throat with both hands and slammed her upright against the wall.

It was then that he saw the blood gushing from his left forearm and felt the pain.

Her second shot had found a home.

Even with the vise of his fingers at her throat, she kicked upward, trying to find his crotch with her knees.

"Be still!" he rasped, his face practically mashed against hers. "If you don't, I'll snap your neck like a twig!"

"*Basta!*" she managed to croak, even while relaxing in his grip.

"It's Lupe de Varga, isn't it?" No answer. "Did he call you Manda? Was that his little lover's name for you?"

"Yes."

"You set him up in Italy, didn't you. The whole business with the Red Brigade back then was a setup to get him out of the way, wasn't it?"

She didn't have to answer. He could see the truth of his words in her eyes.

"Didn't you know he was alive, that he had survived that fire in San Remo?"

"No."

"Why did he hire me to waste you, rather than just do it himself?"

She ignored his question and retaliated with one of her own.

"Who are you? How do you know so much . . . ?"

"Do you want to live or die?" Carter growled, cutting her off. "I want something you've got. You can live until I get it."

Suddenly she brought her claws into play again, this time

digging deeply into Carter's left arm right over the wound.

The pain was instantaneous and, for a brief second, almost blinding. Carter let out a guttural growl and instantly loosened his hold on her throat.

Armanda was across the room like a shot, falling to her knees, her hands finding and grasping the little automatic.

The slight dizziness still gripped Carter, but he managed to lurch toward her. His plan was to smash her to the floor with his superior weight, but again she was quicker than he thought.

She rolled sideways and, like a trained acrobat—or guerrilla fighter—came to her feet.

He crashed to the floor and rolled to his back.

There was little—probably no—chance now. She stood five feet from him, both hands holding the gun straight out from her heaving breasts. The tiny, dark hole of the automatic's muzzle was pointed straight at his belly.

Odd, Carter thought, how weirdly beautiful she is with blood dripping from her chin, her hair a tangled raven mass, defiance in her eyes, and sweat glistening on her naked, rippling body.

"Who are you?"

"Nicholas . . ."

"Who are you!" she shouted, her knuckles growing a little whiter on the trigger. "You know too much to be just a hired killer!"

And then he knew.

She was mad . . . mad as only a fanatic can be mad.

"I will not kill you quickly, you know. I will shoot you in the stomach first. It will burn like the fires of hell. And then I will fire into your kneecaps, first one, then the other . . ."

Carter tensed, anticipating the first shot when he said nothing. He would roll right. His left arm had already taken one slug; one more didn't matter that much now. Better in the arm than in the gut.

But he never had to move.

Suddenly the room exploded with sound and the deep valley between Armanda de Nerro's large, conical breasts was no more.

In its place was a huge round cavity exposing blood and bone.

The gun fell from her hands and her eyes rolled up in her head as she pitched forward across Carter's body.

Over her shoulder, in the doorway, he saw a figure in a dark trench coat. Just before his vision was canceled by de Nerro's body, the figure leaned forward and threw something into the room.

Carter got one brief glimpse of a horribly disfigured face with only one working eye. The other was only a white socket in raw flesh.

By the time he had disengaged himself from the bloody mess that had once been Armanda de Nerro, the figure was gone.

It did not take a medical degree to see that the woman was dead. The slug had entered her back squarely between the shoulder blades.

Its exit between her breasts Carter had already seen.

The rest of it was pretty plain as well.

Wilhelmina, gray wisps of smoke still oozing from her barrel, lay in the middle of the floor.

Lupe de Varga had gotten his revenge. Personally.

And at the same time he had framed an outsider, so the insiders within the ETA could never blame him for her death.

Maybe.

Carter grabbed Wilhelmina and bolted for the stairs. He ejected the magazine and found just what he had expected. It was empty.

In case of error, de Varga had not wanted another shell in the Luger to come looking for him.

Carter crossed the courtyard, knowing that there would be

no retaliation on his part. He had barely reached the edge of the cliff when, far below him, he heard the sound of an engine. Seconds later he saw headlights through the snow and the trees. They swung in a U-turn and moved on down the mountain.

Back in the house, Carter started up the stairs only to come to a halt when his eye fell on a foot and part of a leg protruding from under the stairs.

It was Jock Loran, and he had a hole in his chest very similar to one Carter had just seen in the master bedroom.

Neat, he thought, *very neat.* Maybe it could even be construed as an accident of lustful fate: a love triangle.

Back upstairs, he moved through the bedroom into the bath.

He was a mess. Blood had already clotted in the grooves on his cheeks from Armanda's nails.

His arm was throbbing painfully, but the wound had closed over, and it, too, had clotted. The bullet had passed through clean but had left a spongy hole where it had exited.

Quickly, Carter repaired what he could of his face and upended a bottle of shaving lotion over his arm.

If his guess was right, he didn't have one hell of a lot of time.

It was.

He had barely bandaged the arm with torn strips of a pillowcase, when he heard cars gliding into the front courtyard.

Shrugging into a shirt and jacket, he darted momentarily into the hall. The great room below was flickering eerily with revolving blue lights through the window.

Pausing only long enough to grab four fresh magazines for Wilhelmina, Carter ran to the windows. As he stepped from the window to a tall cyprus, he could hear the incessant banging on the front door.

He could almost hear Lupe de Varga's voice straining over

a telephone wire to the local *policía*: "I was just driving past when I heard what I'm sure was gunfire. Can you imagine? In our quiet little country . . . *gunfire*? I know it is probably impossible, but I think you should investigate . . ."

Probably the only reason Carter had the time he did now to work his way down the tree to the ground was the improbability of it all.

Gunshots in Andorra? Crime—even murder—in this crime-free little paradise?

It was ten-to-one that they had discussed it at the police station for a good twenty minutes before deciding to investigate.

Nevertheless, it would be Carter's ass in the soup when they found two very dead expatriates, and one very missing.

Once on the ground, he worked his way along the ridge line to the corner of the house.

The side leading to the drive was clear, but the blue lights were still dancing at the front in the courtyard.

Going down to Andorra-la-Vella via the road was out of the question. Overland by foot, with the snow and the nearly straight-up-and-down precipice, was equally out.

There was only one way.

Carefully, Carter moved along the side of the house until he was directly across from the garage.

He could hear raised, angry voices shouting from the upstairs windows down to the courtyard.

Taking a deep breath, he darted across the open space and ran into the gaping, open door of the garage. By feel he made his way to the rear and the ski locker he knew was there.

Five minutes later, shod in ski boots, his street shoes tied around his neck, he slipped through the rear door of the garage.

Two thousand feet directly below him lay the lights of Andorra-la-Vella.

As quietly as possible, he clamped boots to skis and poled to the very edge.

His vision was about forty yards, and his left arm hurt like hell.

At least one good thing, he thought. *My tracks will be covered ten minutes after I make them.*

Slowly he eased over the rim, and within seconds he was rocketing down the side of the mountain at better than sixty miles per hour.

TWELVE

Nick Carter dumped the ski boots and skis in a large garbage bin and replaced the boots with his street shoes.

He emerged from a ravine behind a long row of hotels at the dark end of Les Escaldes. Gingerly, he walked parallel to the main street a hundred yards to his right.

Avenue el Pico was a tiny side street of shops and apartment houses. Louisa's hotel was on the corner of the main street and el Pico.

Carter stood, the snow turning his head and shoulders white, at the dead end of el Pico.

Between him and the hotel were four wide apartment buildings. There was no way he dared walk boldly through the hotel lobby by himself up to Louisa's room. There were only two ways: over the roofs or with Louisa's help.

He decided to try the latter first and crossed the street to a cellar beer garden. Just inside the door was a narrow hall with coats lining the walls on both sides.

Carter fingered through them until he found a high-collared topcoat approximately his size. He tugged it on and pushed through the door into the main room.

It was full, mostly youths around long, bare wooden tables. There was much laughter and clanking of heavy beer

mugs as Carter pulled the fur collar up around his mutilated
face and made his way through the tables toward a sign
marked *Teléfono*.

It was perfect: a wall phone near a rear exit.

He dialed the hotel, and a sleepy-voiced concierge
answered on the eighth ring.

"*Señorita Louisa Juaneda, por favor.*"

"*Uno momento.*"

Carter fidgeted as the phone in Louisa's room rang. Twice,
men passed within three feet of him on their way to the john.

Tonight, Carter thought, it would be just his luck that the
real owner of the coat he wore would have bladder problems.

"There is no answer, *señor.*"

"*Gracias.*"

It took him another two minutes to find the number of the
club.

"Cabaret Amour."

"*Sí,* I would like to speak to Señorita Juaneda, *por favor.*"

"Employees cannot receive calls."

"This is important . . . an emergency."

"She is onstage."

"Can you give her a message?"

"I have no pencil."

Carter's fingers tingled. He could feel them curling around
the man's neck.

"I told you, this is an . . ."

The line went dead.

Carter cursed and checked his watch.

It would be at least another two hours, maybe more, before
Louisa would leave the club.

He couldn't be on the streets for two hours, particularly in
this cold with his head swimming.

He had to get under cover, and quick.

Not wanting to expose himself in the cellar room again, he

darted through the rear exit door and skirted the building until he was back on Avenue el Pico.

Slowly he lit a cigarette and cupped it in his hands as he carefully studied the four buildings leading to the hotel.

If he could only get one of those roofs . . .

"Perdóneme."

Carter had been standing directly in front of a bakery shop door. He moved aside as a bent old woman passed him. A set of keys jingled in her hand, and three sacks of groceries were cradled in her arms.

She was halfway up the stoop of the end apartment house when Carter sprinted after her. By the time he reached her, she had unlocked the door and was struggling to tug it open.

"Allow me, *señora.*"

She stepped through without a word. When Carter offered to step in behind her, she whirled in the threshold, belligerently blocking his way.

"Mi amigo . . ." Carter said, gesturing up the stairs.

She growled back at him in a guttural speech he could not understand and gestured toward a bank of buzzers head-high outside the door.

When he smiled and started in anyway, she placed a well-aimed kick at his shin and pulled the door closed behind her. A finger, prominent with swollen knuckles, pointed again at the buzzers, and her seamed face glowered at him through the glass.

"You are a nasty old bitch," Carter whispered.

She nodded, turned, and began hobbling up the stairs.

Carter waited until she was out of sight, and then began randomly pushing all the buttons.

Nothing.

He moved back to the sidewalk and up the street to the next apartment house.

This time he got several vocal replies.

"It is I, José Cartero. I am so sorry, but I have left my key in my flat again. If you would . . ."

The door was still buzzing angrily as Carter hit the stairs four steps at a time. There was a pull-down trapdoor above the top-floor landing, complete with a narrow ladder.

In no time he was back in the snow, sprinting across the roofs.

The hotel was a floor taller than the roof of the last apartment, but it was equipped with an old-style, pull-down fire escape. It was the way of European buildings built close together. You could go from building to building, but not down the front or rear on the outside.

The trapdoor ladder was the same in the hotel. From the top floor, he avoided the elevator and took the stairs. On the third floor he searched for 312 and quickly found it.

There were two locks. One was a turnkey beneath the knob, and the other was a newly installed deadbolt in the panel above it.

Carter ran Hugo's blade through the crack and down. The deadbolt had not been locked. The bolt on the turnkey responded to a gentle shaking of the door. Slowly he was able to inch it open with the blade of the stiletto.

Once inside, he closed and, with a sigh of relief, locked the door behind him.

There were two rooms: a living room and a tiny bedroom alcove behind a set of bedraggled, tattered curtains.

Shunning any light, Carter searched until he found a bottle and a glass. It was gin, but at that moment he couldn't have cared less.

The radio was in the alcove on a tiny stand. He whirled the knob until he found Radio Andorra, poured a full glass of the gin, and sprawled across the bed to wait.

"Nick! Nick!"

The voice oozed down to him, and mentally he tried to

swim up to meet it. It was difficult, very difficult. His arms didn't seem to want to swim, and his mind was in a fog.

Again the voice, oddly familiar, tried to reach him. But only when it was coupled with an iron band gripping his left arm did he respond.

Like a shot he came to an upright position, at the same time flailing out with his arm. This lasted for a few seconds, until a bolt of pain flew from his left arm clear across his body to the fingertips of his right hand and back up to numb his brain.

Like a deflated balloon he crumpled back to the eiderdown quilt and struggled to lift his eyelids.

Louisa Juaneda's dark, flashing eyes and smoldering features came into focus above his face.

"Jesus, I didn't know it was you. I almost skewered you with this before I realized!"

Carter blinked once and saw what could have been Hugo's gleaming twin in her hand.

"What happened?"

"It's a long story. Where's the bottle of gin?"

"You spilled it all over the bed. I have another." She moved quickly across the room and returned, pouring. "Here."

He took half the glass in one swallow, allowed the liquid to burn away the pain in his arm, and then again found her face with his now focused eyes.

"Armanda . . ."

"I know. It's on the radio and all over town."

"And the country." Carter shrugged, drinking again. "It's a small country. Are they looking for me?"

"In every trash can. What happened?"

Briefly, in short, staccato sentences, Carter relayed the night's events, not leaving out a single, gruesome detail.

To Louisa's credit, she listened raptly and did not blink even when he described the picture of Armanda de Nerro being blown apart right before his eyes.

"Are you sure it was de Varga?"

"It stands to reason. It couldn't be anybody else. And the face I saw in the doorway looked like it was a refugee from a burning building."

Carter tried to rise, and again the pain held him motionless a few inches off the bed.

"What is it?"

"A slight hole, somewhere in there," he replied, vaguely pointing with his right hand toward his left arm.

Deftly Louisa removed the fur-collared topcoat and snapped on a bedside lamp.

"Oh, my God . . ."

Carter looked down. The wound had opened up again, and the sleeve of his jacket was dark red from elbow to wrist.

"Get it off," he groaned. "Cut it with a knife."

Carefully she slit the seam at his shoulder and rolled the sopping cloth down and over his hand.

"I think I'm going to be sick."

"Can you wait five minutes? Where's the can?"

"This way."

She slid her shoulders under his right arm and guided him across the living room to a door he had not noticed when he first entered. Inside, she snapped on the light and stayed behind him, carefully averting her eyes from his arm.

"Grab one of those towels," Carter said, gritting his teeth and upending the bottle of gin over his arm, carefully leaving some to drink.

"Now what?" she asked.

"Sponge it off with the towel. Got any bandages around here?"

"I can make some."

"Do that," he said, swallowing a finger and a half and staggering after her into the living room.

He lay back on a sofa, measuring the remainder of the gin

between his lips as Louisa carefully bound the raw, ugly wound.

"Now," he said, "what have you got for me? And let's hope it's good."

She stood and moved across the room. Quickly she tugged a bureau from the wall, reached behind it, and withdrew a manila envelope. Seated beside him again, she extracted the contents of the envelope and spread everything on the coffee table before them.

"Here is a list of all the architects, construction engineers, and building contractors that match the list of buildings constructed or under construction that you gave me."

"And . . . ?"

"*Nada,*" she said, then quickly added with a smile, "But . . ."

"The buildings I gave you were new structures. I left out renovations . . . right?"

The smile of satisfaction faded slightly from Louisa's face, and one eyebrow went up quizzically. "How did you know?"

"Just a guess," Carter wheezed and let the last of the gin trickle onto his tongue. "It's Alain Smythe's villa, isn't it."

"Yes," she said, nodding. "The architecture and structural renovations were done by De Palma and Sons Limited, out of San Sebastian."

"And the connection?"

"De Palma and Sons Limited is a closed corporation, wholly owned by a holding company in Liechtenstein."

"Which couldn't be traced," Carter said wryly.

"That's right."

"But I would lay my good right arm against my bum left one that either Armanda de Nerro or her mother owns the controlling stock in the Liechtenstein corporation."

"But how does Alain Smythe fit in?"

"Good question. I mean to find that out and, if possible, talk to Maria de Nerro."

Louisa's eyes clouded over, and her lower lip curled between her gleaming teeth.

"What is it?" Carter asked.

"She is dead," Louisa replied. "She hanged herself in her hotel room about an hour ago."

Carter smiled and took a swipe at his forehead with his good hand. "They don't waste time, do they? Another good bet is that now Lupe de Varga knows what we know. Did you find anything on the two Americans?"

"Perhaps one . . . the architect."

"Greenspan?"

"Yes. One of the bartenders at the club worked at a small dinner party last night at Smythe's villa. It was for a group of Spaniards. That's how he spotted the American. He only got a brief glimpse of him as he was being put into a car with three of the Spaniards as they were leaving."

"Damn . . ."

"What is it?" Louisa asked, seeing the sudden line of white along Carter's clenched jaw.

"Greenspan's job is done. Chances are, by now, that he's already dead."

"Good God, don't they have any—"

"Conscience?" Carter finished. "None. And if the engineer does his job, we'll find out just how little conscience they have."

"And his job . . . ?"

Carter reached forward and quickly rifled through the huge stack of photographs she had spread on the coffee table. Finally he selected one and moved it between them.

"Smythe's villa?" she asked.

Carter nodded. "You see these turrets and towers?"

"Yes."

"Count them."

Slowly realization flooded Louisa's face. *"Madre de Dios,"* she gasped. "There are eight of them!"

"And the engineer's job is to arm the missiles inside those eight towers."

Carter tugged a pad and pencil before him, and began to scribble. As he did, he barked questions and instructions at Louisa.

"Do you think I'll be safe here until dark tomorrow night?"

"I should think so. Murder is pretty unheard-of in Andorra. I would imagine the police will call in investigative units from either Spain or France for help."

"I'll need fresh dressings for this," he said, indicating his arm, "and a clean suit of clothes. And I want you to leave for Barcelona tonight."

"Barcelona?"

"Yes." He passed the three sheets of paper that he had been scribbling on to Louisa. "Get this message to this guy as fast as you can."

She glanced down at the name on the paper and then looked back up at Carter. "Ramon Cubanez?"

"That's right," Carter replied. "What the hell, it's his show. He might as well get in on the end of it. And there's one thing you can go out and get me right now."

"What?"

"A bottle of scotch. I hate gin."

THIRTEEN

Carter squinted through the crack between the curtains and surveyed the main street of Les Escaldes all the way across the river to Andorra-la-Vella.

It had stopped snowing hours before, around noon. Now the sun was slipping beyond the mountains, turning the day into the orange predecessor of the night.

Louisa had returned from Barcelona at about three with good news. The contact had been made with Cubanez. He had agreed, to the letter, with every request and suggestion Carter had made.

Now it was a waiting game.

It had been a long, harrowing afternoon of boredom for Carter. For hours he had paced, lighting cigarette after cigarette right off the glowing stub of those already smoked down to his fingers.

Through the thin pane of the window he could hear the chatter and laughter of the people on the street below. Most of them were shopkeepers and workers heading home after earning their daily bread.

It gave Carter a strange, momentary longing to be one of them, just another Willie Worker heading home to a pretty wife, a good home-cooked meal, and a few beers and television until bedtime.

"Maudlin," he hissed aloud, "sentimental bullshit!"

He lit another cigarette and plastered his cheek against the window. He craned his neck until he could see the tower of Radio Andorra high atop the Pic Padern Mountain far to his left.

Then his gaze flowed downward until he could distinguish the crenelated walls and soaring towers of Alain Smythe's villa.

Somewhere above or below the villa at that very moment, Ramon Cubanez and one or two hand-picked men were casing the layout.

At least, Carter hoped they were up there.

His watch read 5:40.

It would be a full half hour before complete darkness.

The music on the radio stopped abruptly, and an announcer's voice came droning in with the latest bulletin on the mass killer, Nicholas Carstocus.

Carter smiled.

In Dallas, Texas, or in New York City, a double homicide would rate four lines on page twelve.

In Andorra, it was a "mass murder" that took up the first two pages of the morning paper and rated at least four "update bulletins" per hour on the radio.

Carstocus was still at large somewhere in the country. Then he had slipped over the border into Spain.

The latest update had him spotted simultaneously in Barcelona, Spain, in Perpignan, France, and having a drink in the lounge of a ski lodge in Ronsol, about three and a half miles from where Carter now paced.

There was a tap on the door. Carter grabbed the automatic and pressed his ear against the panel.

"It's me . . . open the door!"

He threw the two locks and yanked the door open. Louisa entered quickly and Carter locked it behind her. When he turned, she had already shed her coat and was halfway out of her skirt and blouse.

"Contact?"

"Yes," she nodded, selecting a dark green, shimmery thing and sliding it over her head. "About ten minutes ago. I'm to meet this Cubanez in the lounge of the Hotel Roc Blanc."

Carter sighed and dropped into a chair. "Then they got in all right."

Again she nodded, applying a brush vigorously to her lustrous hair. "They snowshoed over the Sierra de Enclar from Os de Civis on the Spanish side."

"And the equipment?"

"I don't know," she said, changing her shoes and giving herself a last appraisal in the mirror. "The man who contacted me didn't have much time to talk."

Carter scowled. He had told Cubanez exactly how to get the hardware in—a helicopter drop—and where—in a ravine above the village of Canillo about two and a half miles from the villa.

He only hoped that Cubanez had not taken it upon himself to change Carter's basic plan.

"I'm ready. I should have him back here within the hour."

"Fine," Carter replied, "but make it look good."

"Didn't I make it look good to you?"

"Perfect." He stood and brushed her forehead with his lips. "An hour."

"How's the arm?" she asked, moving to the door.

"Sore as hell, but I can shoot."

"An hour," she said, slipping through the door and closing it behind her.

Carter locked it, then started pacing again.

The decision to make a full-scale, guerrilla-type assault on the villa was his, but it would take some of the edge off an international incident if Cubanez was in on it. As a representative of the Spanish government, Cubanez had no authority in Andorra, but he could take a lot of heat off if something went wrong.

Also, explanations would be more acceptable if they came from him instead of the "mass murderer," Nicholas Carstocus.

But the bottom line was still not to let anything go wrong. If possible, the ideal would be to get in so fast and get it over with so quickly that the Andorrans—police and civilians alike—would never suspect there had been an incident.

Each minute was a passing eternity as night enveloped the peaceful country outside the window.

Carter passed them by imagining the scene in the Roc Blanc lounge. Louisa would be nursing a drink. Cubanez would sidle up to her table and ask if he could join her.

The game would progress just as it does in singles bars all over the world, until Louisa was "seduced."

They would leave the Roc Blanc and walk, arm in arm, a bit unsteadily toward her hotel. In the lobby, the concierge would frown at the young singer's obvious promiscuity, but he would say nothing.

At that moment, Carter heard the elevator at the end of the hall open and Louisa's by now familiar laugh.

Seconds later, her key was turning the deadbolt and Carter was moving into the bedroom alcove, Wilhelmina in hand.

Just in case.

When the door was shut and again securely locked, Carter leathered the Luger and stepped into the room.

"*Buenos noches, mi amigo,*" Cubanez said with a wide grin. "You look like hell."

"*Gracias,*" Carter replied. "And you look like an aging Latin roué."

"Wasn't that the idea?"

"Right. Let's get to work."

"I'll change," Louisa said, darting into the alcove.

From inside the large, fur-trimmed coat he wore, Ramon pulled a series of maps. Then he shed the coat and slid into a chair beside Carter, spreading the maps out on a table.

"You pick some real tricky ones," he said, smoothing out several Polaroids of the Smythe villa and the countryside surrounding it.

"I didn't say it would be a piece of cake," Carter replied. "Before we get into that, what about my hunches?"

"Looks like bull's-eye on every one. Our ferret in the ETA in San Sebastian tells us that the word went out immediately after the news of de Nerro's death hit the streets."

"It is de Varga."

"Right," Cubanez said. "Within the ranks, he claims that he has stayed undercover and hid the fact that he was still alive so he would be free to carry out the ultimate attack on the Spanish government that keeps the Basque people in 'imperialist chains.' "

"And," Carter added, "Armanda de Nerro has only been acting in his stead all this time?"

"Right. Now, because the Spanish government has used the killer, Bluebeard, to assassinate Armanda de Nerro, Lupe de Varga himself has been forced to come into the open to lead the movement."

"Very neat," Carter muttered. "And I fell for it like a ton of bricks."

Cubanez shrugged. "It was well planned and you had no way of knowing. The police and news media are buying the love triangle bit, which also plays into de Varga's plan."

"And the police buying Maria de Nerro's killing as a suicide also plays into his hand."

Cubanez grinned, his stark white teeth gleaming like ivory in his dark face. "But into ours as well. If we pull this off tonight, the whole thing will be dismissed as just another jet-set scandal, and no one will be the wiser that eight nuclear devices have fallen into the hands of fanatic terrorists.''

Carter nodded and rifled quickly through the photos.

"When did de Varga and his crew move into the villa?"

"My guess is within minutes after Armanda de Nerro's murder was broadcast. It was probably easy. Her people thought de Varga was dead. When he turned up alive, knowing the whole blackmail scheme, and de Nerro was dead, they just accepted the new leadership.''

"What about Alain Smythe?" Carter asked, selecting a blowup of the villa proper and studying it with rapt concentration.

"As near as we can tell, it is the same deal as De Palma and Sons Limited in San Sebastian. Smythe came up fast from nowhere. It takes a lot of money to get started in the fashion industry, and even more to branch out into allied businesses like perfume, design endorsements, and the like. Years, usually.''

"And Smythe did it in less than three years," Carter growled.

"Did it big. We have not been able to confirm this, but when we do I imagine we'll find another Liechtenstein holding company behind Alain Smythe Enterprises. Armanda de Nerro was a very organized woman. My guess is that she owned Smythe. He had to go along with this or she could have—how do you say?—pulled the plug on his little empire.''

"Good enough," Carter said. "Let's get to it."

Cubanez arranged maps and pictures in front of them, and started to explain.

The renovations of the villa had been little short of miraculous. To the ordinary eye it appeared that Smythe had

"Good enough. Where's the car?"

"I will take you to it."

Louisa had slipped from the bedroom alcove. She had donned a pair of skintight black jeans, a layer of sweaters, and a heavy leather jacket. Fur-lined boots were on her feet.

Carter started to speak, but she held up her hand.

"I'm going. I've been baring my breasts and playing prostitute up here for six months. Now that it's finally happening, I want to be there!"

Carter looked at Cubanez, who shrugged.

"Ramon, what's the hardware?" Carter growled.

"Czech Skorpions for rapid fire," he said, "and our own Astra three-fifty-sevens for sidearms."

Carter turned to Louisa. "You ever fire an Astra?"

"No."

"The recoil can break your wrist."

"I'll use two hands," she replied.

"So be it," Carter said. "Let's go."

"See you on the mountain!" Cubanez said, going through the door.

FOURTEEN

A stiff breeze blew down off the mountains as the little car climbed steadily upward past the tall radio tower. Snow swirled in hazy gusts, forcing Carter to turn on the wipers every couple of minutes.

Beside him, in the passenger seat, Louisa sat stoically, staring straight ahead.

"Scared?"

"Yes."

"Good. You wouldn't be human if you weren't."

"How is Cubanez getting up here?"

"A jeep," Carter replied, "from the other side of Canillo."

A last hairpin turn, and the barricades denoting the road's end came up in the headlights' twin beams. Carter nuzzled the front bumper against them and killed the engine.

"We walk from here."

From the car's trunk he rescued two pairs of snowshoes and instructed Louisa how to lace them onto her boots.

"Ready?" he asked at last.

"I suppose so."

"Let's go."

The snow was powder for about eight inches down and

packed solid underneath. It made for fast moving. Less than a half hour later, they were high on the mountain and moving across its peak.

"Much farther?" she asked from behind him in an only slightly breathless voice.

"Those trees, there. Hold up!"

Carter took a penlight from his pocket and blinked its beam three quick times toward the trees.

The answer came back at once.

"C'mon!"

They trudged the remaining forty yards and found themselves in a makeshift camp.

"You made good time," Cubanez said. "Your equipment is there."

Carter checked the load in a UZ61 Skorpion, loosened the lanyard, and wriggled it across his back. He then hooked two spare magazines to his pockets and adjusted a pair of goggles around his head.

He noticed, out of the corner of his eye as he stepped into his skis, that Louisa was duplicating his every move.

The last thing he did was to buckle on the holster, Western-style, that held the heavy Astra .357. He still had Wilhelmina under his left armpit, but for that night's work the Astra would better serve the purpose.

One slug in a crowd from the powerful handgun could go right through one body and fell a second.

"Ready?" Cubanez asked, joining them.

"Got it," Carter replied, looking to Louisa, who nodded.

"Let's go. The others are down below on the ridge, ready to move out."

The skis made a faint hissing sound as they zigzagged down the short slope and came out on a narrow plateau high above the valley.

Directly below them was the radio tower, and far below it

were the lights of Andorra-la-Vella and Les Escaldes.

Somewhere in between was the villa.

Six men stood on the edge of the precipice on skis. All of them were armed and ready.

Four others in black suits, looking like dark moths with the large black wings of their hang gliders poised above them, stood to the rear. All of them were poised in a crouch, ready to run off the top of the mountain.

The top man in command under Cubanez was introduced as Alfredo. He was a hulking bear of a man, made bigger by the harness draped around his body. He had shaggy black hair, dead eyes, and deep scars on both sides of his face.

Carter did not offer his own name, and no one asked.

Carter cased the others and found them to be stamped from the same mold as Alfredo. Cubanez had already told him that they were a crack antiterrorist team, and that was good enough for him.

There were no handshakes and only a bare vocal greeting before they got down to business.

"There is an American in there. His name is Lorenzo Montegra. If possible, I want him kept alive. He is an engineer and will know how to dismantle the missiles. That will make the cleanup later quicker and easier."

"*Señor?*" It was Alfredo.

"*Sí?*"

"This man Montegra . . . has he already armed the missiles?"

"We don't know," Carter replied, pausing to let his words sink in. "It's possible. That's why, as soon as you knock out the guns on the roof, you must move down to the tower doors as soon as possible to stop anyone from entering."

"I have briefed them all," Cubanez added, "on the villa floor plan from the master in the city files."

Carter nodded. "That floor plan should be exact, except

for the alterations inside the towers.''

Again Carter paused, looking at each man in turn before speaking again.

''This must be done as quickly and cleanly as possible. Also, these men are fanatics. I have no doubts that they are prepared to die to the last man.''

''Then, *señor*,'' Alfredo growled, ''that is what they shall do.''

''All right,'' Cubanez said, ''everybody stay in radio contact. Alfredo . . .''

The big man growled something to his three comrades, and, as one, they sprinted toward the edge of the cliff.

As silent as death they sailed out into the night sky, and within seconds they were lost in the inky blackness.

''Our turn,'' Cubanez said. ''Single file . . . I will lead.''

Carter turned to Louisa. ''Stay close to me.''

''Don't worry, I will!''

One by one, over they went.

Cubanez had the difficult job leading the way. The others, crouched low, had only to follow his track.

On purpose, Cubanez swung the column in wide arcs. Because of this it was almost a half hour before they broke through the trees and found themselves in a wide field to the rear of the villa.

''Skis off!'' Cubanez hissed. ''We walk in from here!''

The villa squatted like a huge mound of dark stone about two hundred yards in front of them.

The field itself was used as a pasture in the summertime. It was dotted with great, high boulders and groups of pine and scrub trees.

They moved forward, again in single file. Halfway across, the trees thinned out and Cubanez picked up the pace.

Now and then Carter glanced up, his eyes scanning the night sky for the men riding the gliders.

He could see nothing. It was pitch-black, so black that the outline of the villa itself against the sky could barely be discerned.

Even as chill as it was, perspiration gleamed on Carter's face. It came from anticipation as well as the exertion of the march.

"Hold it!" Cubanez whispered.

The column stopped and fanned out behind him and Carter.

They were forty yards short of the moat and the high, stone walls of the villa. Directly in front of them was a long, seemingly unending line of huge rocks.

"Is there a path between or over those boulders?" Carter asked.

"Yes," Cubanez replied. "I spotted it with binoculars this afternoon."

"It will be as slick as glass with this new snow."

"I know," Cubanez nodded and motioned up two men from the column.

One of them carried a canvas pack, the other something that looked like two aluminum poles.

"It's a lightweight loading chute," Cubanez explained. "It extends in width and length, and weighs next to nothing."

"To walk the moat?" Carter ventured.

"Exactly. Here's your pack. You are the bomber expert. I will position the men."

Carter grinned and accepted the pack as Cubanez slipped away. From it he took a hot-shot battery, two coils of wire, and a bundle tightly wrapped in oilskin.

"What's that?" Louisa asked, peering over Carter's shoulder.

"Good old-fashioned dynamite," he replied. "It makes the kind of boom everyone around here is used to hearing."

"My God, you'll blow up the whole villa!"

"Would that I could," Carter said as he broke the ties on the wire and started wrapping the two coils together with a loose twist.

Then he opened the end of the bundle and carefully inserted a fuse into the center stick of dynamite. This done, he tied the end of the wires to the coil he had already scraped clean. Then he uncrossed the opposite ends of the coil wires and handed them to Louisa.

"Hold these . . . and keep your hands clear of that battery. Ramon?"

"Here," came the reply out of the darkness, and then the man himself materialized.

"How close are we?"

"The jeep just checked in. They are in place. All we need now is the word from Alfredo."

It came five minutes later when the little light on top of the two-way in Cubanez's hand glowed red. He opened the channel and spoke.

"Go ahead."

"Alfredo here. The roof is secure. Six dead, no alert. We're moving down to the tower doors now."

"Good enough." He closed the channel and glanced up at Carter. "Ready?"

"Follow me over," Carter replied. "You carry the battery. Louisa, the wires!"

In a half crouch, with his feet widely spaced and the dynamite pack in one hand, he scaled the boulder and slid down the other side on his butt.

It was about twenty yards to the moat, and by the time he got there two men were already extending the aluminum chute. One end of it fell silently in the snow on the other side, and Carter barely missed a beat as his feet hit the chute.

It took him a full two minutes to find a depression between

the phony stone and the concrete foundation. When he did, he securely lodged the lethal pouch and retreated back across the moat, playing the wire out behind him.

The two men pulled the ladder a safe distance, then slid in between the rocks.

When Carter was again squatting between Louisa and Cubanez, he took the battery.

"I'll need a little light for safety's sake, but shield it."

Cubanez cupped a penlight between his hands and pointed the beam down at the battery.

Carter attached one of the two coils to the battery terminal. Carefully he kinked the second loose wire away from the terminal and looked up.

"Ramon . . ."

"*Sí?*"

"Your men know enough to keep their heads down?"

"Oh, yes. And they know the groups they split into when they get inside. I've rehearsed it all, over and over again, with each one of them."

"Good. Louisa?"

"*Sí?*"

"Lie flat and cover your head with your rifle and your arms. When this goes, there's going to be rock and concrete flying all over hell around here. Here we go!"

Carter pressed the wire to the second terminal, and the night was filled with sound.

The explosion was deafening. Rocks, dirt, and hunks of concrete filled the air. The wall of boulders blocked most of the debris, but a few fragments must have gotten through.

As Carter lifted his head from his arms, he heard moaning just behind him.

One of the men was cursing and trying to apply a makeshift tournequet to his arm. He saw Carter's questioning glance and flashed him a thumbs-up sign.

"Let's go!" Carter hissed when the last of the falling rocks clattered back to earth.

Sliding down the other side of the mound of boulders, they heard a second explosion far in the distance, quickly followed by a third.

Across the moat, there was a gaping twenty-foot-wide hole in the wall of the villa. Inside, Carter could see electrical sparks flying all over the place.

"Watch the bare wires when you go through!" he shouted just as he gained the edge of the moat.

The two ladder bearers were on the ball. The aluminum chute was already stretched across the moat, and they were holding it steady as Carter's boots hit it.

Two seconds later he was through the hole and into the kitchen. He could hear the jeep-mounted .50-caliber opening up in front and the footsteps of the others behind him.

Several exposed wires were doing wild things along one wall. They left sparks and the beginnings of tiny fires where they skipped. Finally two of them collided, and the lights went off when a breaker somewhere hit.

"Let's go!" Carter rasped, unlimbering the Skorpion from across his back.

There was an exit to the right and one to the left.

Carter saw Cubanez go through the right as he burst through the left, with Louisa and two of the others right behind him.

He found himself in the great room of the villa.

Two men were running wildly down the stairway. When they saw the raiding party, they tried to swing the machine pistols bumping their sides into action.

Without breaking stride, Carter sprayed them both. At the same time he heard firing from the other wing of the ground floor, telling him that Cubanez was engaged.

"Two of you take the front door! They'll be coming in

from the courtyard. You . . . cover our asses!''

Louisa was already bounding up the stairs. Carter took off after her. Halfway up, there was a single shot and then a burst from the Skorpion.

''Louisa . . . !''

''I'm all right!'' she yelled, her voice already fading down a hall.

Carter headed up, full tilt. At the top he nearly tripped over a body and chalked up one for Louisa.

She obviously knew how to use the Skorpion and wasn't afraid to.

The lights came back on when Carter entered the hall. Louisa was at the far end.

Carter was about to sprint after her, when a door midway between them burst open and his old buddy, Ramos, stepped out. He was facing Louisa, bringing up the ugly snout of a machine pistol.

''Ramos!''

The man spun toward Carter just in time to catch a five-shot burst from Carter's Skorpion. The slugs stitched across his chest, throwing him flat against the wall. He paused there, upright for a second, and then slowly slid down, leaving the wallpaper behind him crimson with gore.

''I told you I'd kill you, you son of a bitch,'' Carter hissed as he broke into a run.

He joined Louisa, and together they went from room to room.

The firing from below and outside the house had abated. What he could hear was an occasional staccato burst that was unmistakably fire from an UZ61.

That meant that the war was nearly over, and their side had won.

Then, from behind a huge, paneled door at the end of the hall, there was the boom of a shotgun.

"Louisa . . . do you remember what's in there?"

"Upstairs library, I think."

"Cover me!"

The door opened just as Carter reached it, and he smashed directly into Lupe de Varga. He was brandishing a sawed-off double-barreled Winchester.

De Varga tried to bring the barrel around, but before he could, Carter had a grip on it. Carter wrenched it from the scar-faced man's hands just as de Varga's finger squeezed the trigger.

A hot blast seared by Carter's neck and shoulder, and the buckshot made a mess of the oak door.

"Forget it, Lupe, you've had it. The war's over."

De Varga didn't think so.

He made a grab with both hands for the Skorpion resting across Carter's chest.

"Damned fool," Carter hissed, reversing the Winchester and driving the heavy stock into the man's guts.

De Varga groaned and doubled over.

Carter dropped the Winchester, stepped in fast, and straightened the man with a hard right to the side of his head.

He tried to whirl away, but Carter stopped him with a crushing heel to his instep. At the same time, he buried his fist wrist deep in the man's gut, and the fight was over.

Carter easily manhandled him into a chair and pulled the monstrous Astra from its holster at his hip.

"Where's Lorenzo Montegra?"

Silence.

"Have you armed any of the missiles yet?"

More silence, not even a look.

"Nick . . ."

It was Cubanez. Carter turned to face him. He stood in the doorway holding a sniveling Alain Smythe up by his collar. Louisa was just behind them.

"Any casualties?"

"None," Cubanez said. "Two wounded, neither seriously."

"And theirs?"

"Eleven dead. No one got away. I found this one hiding in a closet."

"Montegra?"

"No sign. The towers are secure. This one says he knows where they kept the arming devices."

"You pig!" de Varga shouted and lunged toward Smythe.

Carter caught him full in the face with the butt of the Skorpion and knocked him back into the chair.

He turned back to Smythe. Over the man's shoulder, he saw Louisa wince.

"Where's Montegra?"

"I don't know, I swear it," Smythe whimpered and then started crying. "They made me do everything. I swear I didn't—"

"Get him out of here and gather up the arming devices!"

When the door was closed, Carter turned back to de Varga.

With quick, deft fingers he went through the man's pockets. Then, using Hugo, he ripped his clothing apart.

He found what he wanted between the two halves of his leather belt.

"Are these the ETA numbered accounts in Switzerland and Liechtenstein?"

"Who are you?"

"I'm not Nicholas Carstocus."

"That figures," de Varga said weakly. "Can you be bought?"

"No."

The man was silent.

"Where's Montegra!"

"Over there, behind the screen."

Carter crossed the room and whipped the screen aside.

Lorenzo Montegra was tied hand and foot to a chair. Half his chest was blown away.

Then Carter remembered the shotgun blast he had heard.

"He was a casualty," de Varga growled. "A casualty of a war of liberation."

"Oh, yeah?"

"I gave him a choice . . . arm the missiles or die. He chose to die."

Silently Carter cursed. If he had been five minutes faster up the stairs. . . .

He walked to the door and turned.

"Casualty, huh?"

"One more does not matter in our struggle," de Varga said, his one good eye blazing at Carter from his mangled face.

"Then join the list," Carter hissed.

The Astra sounded like a Howitzer in the small room. The slug took de Varga dead center in the chest, sending both his lifeless body and the chair clear across the room.

The tower cribs were architectural marvels. The entire inner cones of the towers were elevators. When the missiles were ready for firing, the elevator would go up, literally pushing the small tower room and the roof off.

"Think they would have fired them?" Cubanez asked as they finished inspecting the last one and made their way toward the roof.

"Yes, I think they would have," Carter replied.

He took the black case containing the firing devices from Cubanez and passed him the two slips of paper he had taken from de Varga's belt.

"You contacted Julio Mendez?"

Cubanez nodded. "He will cooperate fully."

"I'm sure Smythe can help you get into most of those

accounts. Perhaps Mendez can use the money to turn the ETA into something that the Basques can believe in.''

"Perhaps," Cubanez said. "But who knows?"

In the distance they could hear heavy trucks rumbling up the mountain. Within twenty-four hours, the missiles would be completely broken down and stored in the trucks. Then they would be driven into Spain and quietly shipped back to the States.

"We've rounded up the De Palma and Sons people in San Sebastian," Cubanez said, "and just about everybody is talking."

"How widespread was it?" Carter asked.

"Pretty much as you figured. Armanda de Nerro had cells in Italy, France, and all over Spain. Security has been alerted in all those countries, and they're mopping up."

"With any luck," Carter growled, "maybe we can get a Soviet connection."

"I doubt it. They finance and train, but they are very careful about staying in the background."

Two men moved past them to the waiting chopper. They carried Lorenzo Montegra in a makeshift body bag.

Louisa stepped out onto the roof, and Carter crossed to meet her.

"Where do you go?" she asked.

"Paris first, to lay Nicholas Carstocus to rest at last, and then . . ." He shrugged.

She kissed him gently on the cheek, started to turn, and paused.

"Somewhere out there is another Lupe de Varga," she said.

Carter nodded. "You can bet on it."

"Then we'll probably meet again."

"I hope not," Carter said, managing a wan smile.

He squeezed her hand, turned, and walked to the waiting chopper. The rotor was starting to roll around as he climbed the ladder and threw a final salute to Cubanez.

When he was secure in the bucket seat, he relaxed at last . . .

And remembered . . .

The address and phone number in Avignon . . .

No, let her forget.

Then he remembered another phone number . . . of an answering service in Washington.

Her name was Delores, and with any luck she would be at one of the watering holes on this side of the pond—probably Monte Carlo.

With any luck.

He would call from Paris.

By the time the chopper cleared the roof, Nick Carter was smiling.

DON'T MISS THE NEXT NEW NICK CARTER SPY THRILLER

DAY OF THE MAHDI

Two men sprang from each side of the bulldozer. The four were Bedouins, robed in white, swinging long swords that gleamed menacingly in the gloom.

There is an instant of shock after the completely unexpected happens. It can stretch to thirty seconds or more for the average person. Long enough for a fatal automobile accident. Long enough for a crippling fall down a cliff. Long enough for a bulldozer going at full speed to crush all in its path.

The Bedouins' berserk cries swelled in the air.

The bulldozer's blade advanced.

Nick Carter moved first.

With his lightning-quick overhand, Carter sent Hugo slicing through the darkness and into the carotid artery of the bulldozer's driver. The driver shot up out of his seat, desperately trying to hold his throat together. Blood gushed out in a geyser that soaked the white-robed driver and covered the steering wheel. The bulldozer stalled and stopped.

The Bedouins screamed and swung their long swords above their heads.

"Religious fanatics, old boy!" Cecil Young shouted and pulled a service revolver from his burnoose.

A Bedouin brought his long sword down and Cecil Young moved just in time so that he lost only his revolver.

Carter kicked the Bedouin in the belly. He felt the satisfactory crush of stomach and intestines. The Bedouin squealed and doubled over. Carter smoothly swiveled away. Cecil Young pulled a metal drawer from the desk and slammed the Bedouin's face to the floor. Blood spread into a lake around the head.

Carter moved in on the other three, dodging the wide-swinging swords, and jammed his fist into the groin of one Bedouin followed by a brutal upper-cut that knocked the Bedouin deep into the confetti of the bulldozer's blade.

Cecil Young picked up the first Bedouin's sword and, swinging it above his head as if he were born to it, bellowed in Arabic:

"There is no god but God! Muhammad is the messenger of God!"

The last two Bedouins spun to attack Cecil.

Carter yanked down the black headband of one and snapped it across the neck in a powerful contraction that broke the man's voicebox. The Bedouin tore at the headband, his mouth open in a soundless scream. Carter threw him out the window.

The bulldozer roared to life and jerked toward them. The Bedouin who had been thrown into the blade's confetti had crawled up and now sat in the dead driver's seat, his face bruised and ugly with hate as he drove the big machine down on them.

—From *Day of the Mahdi*
A New Nick Carter Spy Thriller
From Charter in July

☐ 08374-9	**THE BUDAPEST RUN**	$2.50
☐ 14217-6	**THE DEATH DEALER**	$2.50
☐ 14220-6	**DEATH ISLAND**	$2.50
☐ 14172-2	**THE DEATH STAR AFFAIR**	$2.50
☐ 29782-X	**THE GOLDEN BULL**	$2.25
☐ 47183-8	**THE LAST SUMARAI**	$2.50
☐ 57502-1	**NIGHT OF THE WARHEADS**	$2.50
☐ 58866-2	**NORWEGIAN TYPHOON**	$2.50
☐ 65176-3	**THE PARISIAN AFFAIR**	$2.50
☐ 71133-2	**THE REDOLMO AFFAIR**	$1.95
☐ 71228-2	**THE REICH FOUR**	$1.95
☐ 95305-0	**THE YUKON TARGET**	$2.50

Prices may be slightly higher in Canada.

Available at your local bookstore or return this form to:

 CHARTER BOOKS
Book Mailing Service
P.O. Box 690, Rockville Centre, NY 11571

Please send me the titles checked above. I enclose _____ Include 75¢ for postage and handling if one book is ordered; 25¢ per book for two or more not to exceed $1.75. California, Illinois, New York and Tennessee residents please add sales tax.

NAME _____

ADDRESS _____

CITY _____ STATE/ZIP _____

(allow six weeks for delivery.)   A8